WYOMING SUNRISE
PREQUEL

Love's New Beginnings

PENNY ZELLER

WYOMING SUNRISE
PREQUEL

Love's New Beginnings

PENNY ZELLER

Maplebrook

Love's New Beginnings

Copyright © 2022 by Penny Zeller

www.pennyzeller.com

www.pennyzeller.wordpress.com

Published by Maplebrook Publishing

Christian Historical Romance

Cover design and Editing by Mountain Peak Edits & Design

All scripture quotations are taken from the King James Version of the Bible.

Print ISBN: 978-1-957847-03-0

Books by Penny Zeller

Maplebrook Publishing

Standalone Novels
Love in Disguise

Wyoming Sunrise Series
Love's New Beginnings (Prequel)
Forgotten Memories
Dreams of the Heart

Love Letters from Ellis Creek Series
Love from Afar
Love Unforeseen
Love Most Certain

Love in Chokecherry Heights Series
Henry and Evaline (Prequel)
Love Under Construction

Standalone Novellas
Freedom's Flight

Horizon Series
Over the Horizon

Whitaker House Publishing
Montana Skies Series
McKenzie
Kaydie
Hailee

Barbour Publishing
Love from Afar (The Secret Admirer Romance Collection)
Freedom's Flight (The Underground Railroad Brides Collection)

Beacon Hill Press (Nonfiction)
77 Ways Your Family Can Make a Difference

To everyone who has ever wondered or questioned if they are where God has called them to be.

Casting all your care upon him; for he careth for you.
~ 1 Peter 5:7

CHAPTER ONE

WYOMING TERRITORY, 1869

LYDIE BEAUCHAMP STALKED DOWN the dusty streets of Prune Creek, her skirt swishing against her ankles.

Usually she was a calm and mild-mannered young woman.

Usually.

But not today.

Today, decorum was the last thing on her mind.

Both Aunt Fern and Aunt Myrtle would have her hide and then some if they knew what she was about to do. "So uncharacteristic of you, child," Aunt Fern would say.

"You really ought to remember the proper way to handle disputes," Aunt Myrtle would admonish.

Even with the thoughts of how her aunts might respond *if* they found out, Lydie's fury was about to spring to life.

Lydie passed the barber shop, livery, blacksmith, and the church that doubled as a schoolhouse. She marched past the bank, saloon, and post office. Until she reached the mercantile where *he* stood loading items into his saddle bag.

She wished she was spunky like Aunt Myrtle, rather than quiet and reserved.

*Although...*quiet and reserved might not be the words *he* would use to describe her once she unleashed her thoughts about the whole ordeal.

"Miss Beauchamp, of what do I owe the pleasure?" The man in his forties with a black handlebar mustache removed his hat, revealing a large balding spot in his otherwise graying black hair.

"You know exactly why I'm here, Mr. Wilkins." Lydie did her best to raise her voice, but it still came out squeaky like that of a young child's. She would need to work on that if she was ever going to be a teacher and deal with wayward pupils.

Mr. Wilkins smirked. "Now, now, young lady. You know full well it wasn't ever going to work between your aunt and me."

"But Aunt Fern moved here to the Wyoming Territory just so the two of you could marry. And now you have called off the wedding two days before the event." She placed her hands on her hips and did her best to glower.

Apparently it was not very convincing, because Mr. Wilkins only laughed.

"South Pass City is calling me." He held a hand to his right ear. "That precious thing called gold is calling me. Prune Creek and being married and settling down with Fern are not."

Lydie had heard of South Pass City and the gold that was to be found in the town a great distance from Prune Creek. But she'd never anticipated Aunt Fern's intended would be drawn into the lure of hunting for it.

Not that she knew Mr. Wilkins well. To the contrary, she'd only met him a month ago when she and her aunts moved from Minnesota to the wilds of the Wyoming Territory.

"You made a vow to marry Aunt Fern. An honorable man never goes back on his word." Why did her voice sound so tinny? She cleared her throat and tried again. "You promised to marry her, settle down with her, and make a life with her in Prune Creek."

Mr. Wilkins shook his head. "She may have misunderstood. Look, Miss Beauchamp, I have a lot of riding ahead of me if I want to make some headway before nightfall. Sorry you're upset and all about Fern, but this is the way it is. She'll find someone else."

But Lydie had an inkling Aunt Fern would never find someone else, for her heart was broken beyond repair.

"But, Mr. Wilkins..."

"No two ways about it, Miss Beauchamp. I'm not staying in Prune Creek and I'm not marrying Fern." He swung a leg over the horse and settled into his saddle.

And then that despicable man rode off heading south.

Her eyes smarted with tears. Not because she had failed at convincing Mr. Wilkins to stay and marry Aunt Fern, but because he had hurt someone Lydie cared about more than life itself.

The thundering sound of the stagecoach rumbling down the road toward town shifted Lydie's focus and she stepped up onto the boardwalk. She closed her eyes as a plume of dust engulfed the air.

Lord, please help Aunt Fern. Help her heart to heal.

Lydie sighed and began her walk toward home before the aunts realized she'd disappeared.

Home.

They'd left behind all they had in Minnesota to chase Aunt Fern's lovelorn dreams. While they hadn't many possessions at their former residence, they *did* have a home in which to reside and the aunts had taken in mending and washing to support themselves. Now here in the Wild West, where outlaws perched on every corner, horse thieves and cattle rustlers were the norm, and nothing refined or cultured existed in the dusty town, their futures appeared bleak.

So much for new beginnings.

They couldn't return to Minnesota, for there was nothing left for them there. No family and no home. Aunt Fern, having so excitedly shared the news with their church friends about marrying a handsome cowboy in the Wild West, would never return to announce her failure.

The single women had swooned at Aunt Fern's exuberance. Aunt Myrtle, who could be quite contrary, supported Aunt Fern to the fullest and agreed the move was best for them all. Lydie figured deep down inside Aunt Myrtle was a romantic at heart, just like her sister.

Lydie sighed. How could they support themselves here? She'd applied for the teaching position at the school to no avail. According to rumors perpetuated by the mercantile owner's wife, Miss Owsten planned to teach until she was ninety-nine. Lydie obviously couldn't wait that long.

The aunts had taken in some mending, but it apparently wasn't a priority here to have clothing in satisfactory condition. Men appreciated the missing buttons on their worn and smelly old shirts. And while men outnumbered the women by a ratio of six to one, none of them were suitable beaus for either of the aunts.

Lydie stepped into the post office. Perhaps one of their Minnesota friends had written to inquire as to their wellbeing. After all, the aunts had declared their move to be one of excitement and adventure. The things written of in dime novels.

"Hello, Miss Beauchamp. How did you know I had a letter for you?" The post office clerk, a man whose name she couldn't recall offhand, reached into one of the slots to retrieve the correspondence.

"You must mean for the aunts?"

"No, this one is addressed to you." The clerk handed her the letter.

Lydie inhaled a sharp breath. Could it be?

Her name, in scrawled and slanted penmanship, peered up at her.

She closed her eyes, breathed a prayer, and released the breath she'd been holding. She couldn't open it. Couldn't. So much depended on the words penned inside.

"Might you open this for me?" Lydie slightly opened one eye and attempted to hand the letter to the clerk.

"Me?" the postal clerk recoiled. "But it is addressed to you." He shook his head. "No, miss, you best open it."

Lydie could just toss the letter in the fireplace tonight and not give it another thought.

Oh, but she would give it another thought. And dwell on it for days, pondering what might have been. Deliberating the words written on the page neatly tucked inside the envelope.

Lord, may Your will be done.

That was a difficult prayer, for Lydie's desire could quite possibly be vastly different than the Lord's plans for her. She debated whether she'd been sincere in the prayer, but recalled last week's sermon about God knowing the hearts of people, even if their prayers indicated otherwise.

Five minutes later, she was on the boardwalk again, still clutching the envelope. A crinkle along the edges testified to her firm, albeit nervous, grasp on it. Finally, she opened the flap, daring herself to scan the words upon the page.

Dear Miss Beauchamp,

I trust this finds you doing well.

I am pleased to announce you have been chosen for the teaching position in Willow Falls. Room and board and a small stipend will be provided, and the first day of school will commence on the second Monday in September.

Please respond posthaste if you are still interested.

Sincerely,

Mr. Morton

School Board Chairman

Lydie's heart raced and she re-read the letter five more times. She'd never met the school board chairman and she'd never been to Willow Falls, a town over the mountain from Prune Creek. But soon she would be the new teacher, and not only the new teacher, but the very *first* teacher.

She held a hand to her bosom. Could she teach? Could she inspire and mold young minds? Could she succeed at this dream of a new beginning in her life? Would the couple with whom she would stay be charitable? Would the kindly townsfolk take pity and give her a second chance if she failed in her attempts?

Would she be able to be away from the aunts?

The latter concerned her the most.

Fear, apprehension, and worry niggled its way into Lydie's heart. Perhaps deciding to be a teacher was not the calling God had placed on her life. Perhaps the letter was intended for someone else.

But sure enough, when she unfolded the stationery and peeked again at the salutation, her name was there amongst the somewhat-messy and overly-slanted penmanship.

There was another matter which demanded her full attention. Whether she should accept the teaching position in Willow Falls or remain in Prune Creek depended on a critical happenstance. She must find a way for the aunts to support themselves. Either that or bring them along with her to Willow Falls.

A new adventure it would be if they all three moved once again to a new town. Aunt Myrtle and Aunt Fern thrived on change. Lydie did not. But it would be a doable adventure if she didn't have to do it alone. Quite possibly there would be a job for them mending and sewing in Willow Falls, although if this was the first time a school teacher was to be hired, the town was likely smaller than Prune Creek. That posed the problem of job opportunities.

Moments later, she returned home, the letter carefully hidden in her bodice. The aunts mustn't know of the teaching position, for if they did, they would encourage her to accept without delay. They'd always been supportive of her dreams and had taken such good care of her in all these years after her parents died.

No, she wouldn't tell them about the acceptance until she had a plan in place. Perhaps she wouldn't even accept the offer to be the first teacher in Willow Falls after all.

Lydie snuck past the aunts and into her meager portion of the log cabin, a miniscule area behind a curtain that provided just enough room for a bed and a bureau. She then proceeded to pace. Three steps to the curtain, three steps to the bed. Then all over again.

"Child, you are about to wear a hole in the floor." Aunt Myrtle's voice rose above the clomp-clomp of Lydie's boots.

"And I see your feet going this way and that," added Aunt Fern, her voice teary. "What has you so jittery and overwrought?"

If only you knew, my dear aunts.

Aunt Myrtle spoke again. "Come out here and have something to eat. I need your help with Aunt Fern."

Lydie wondered what the problem may be with Aunt Fern, but surmised it must have to do with Mr. Wilkins's brash behavior. She tucked the letter inside her bureau beneath her Sunday dress, pushed the curtain aside, and stepped into the humble common area.

Aunt Myrtle sliced a piece of bread. "Care for a sandwich for the noonday meal?" she asked.

A sandwich sounded delicious, although who could eat at a time like this when the very future of three lives teetered on one person's choice? Yet her stomach rumbled, reminding her she hadn't eaten since early that morning. "Yes, thank you."

"Now, Lydie, remind Aunt Fern that nourishment is necessary for survival."

Lydie placed an arm around Aunt Fern. "You know what Aunt Myrtle is saying is true."

"Are you taking sides?" Aunt Fern dabbed at her eyes with a doily.

"Did you mean to wipe your eyes with the doily?" Lydie handed her aunt the checkered handkerchief that rested on the table next to the lace doily.

"Dear me, no." That caused another round of sobs and Lydie regretted her attempts at making light of the situation. She drew Aunt Fern to her, placed her chin on her aunt's head, and did her best to comfort her.

Aunt Myrtle stood with her hands on her hips. "Of course Lydie is taking sides. I'm right in this matter. And *most* matters."

Lydie held her tongue. Aunt Myrtle was a spirited one and most definitely *not* right in most matters. But alas, she cared deeply for her younger sister and only wanted what was best for her.

"Why did we come all this way and leave everything behind? I feel so distraught at the thought of upending our lives like I did. Will you both ever find it in your hearts to forgive me?"

"You're already forgiven, now quit with the nonsense," admonished Aunt Myrtle, always the more practical one.

Lydie patted Aunt Fern's arm. "Of course we forgive you. How were you to know that despicable dolt would cause such an upheaval of the heart?"

"Upheaval of the heart?" Aunt Fern peered up at Lydie through teary eyes. "Wherever did you come up with that phrase, child?"

Lydie loved to read, so it could have been from one of the few novels they owned that she'd recently re-read for the fiftieth time. Or it could have been from her own mind. Not that she would admit it to anyone, but she was a bit on the romantic side. But romance was not something she could discuss at this moment, especially not with Aunt Fern's broken heart. "Not quite sure, Aunt Fern, but I do know that you are such a dear and if you don't receive proper nourishment, you'll waste away to skin and bones and succumb to an early death. Aunt Myrtle and I would forever be in a state of melancholy without you here."

Even to her own ears, Lydie sounded rather dramatic, and she didn't think of herself as the dramatic type. More like a shy and reserved woman with plentiful inner contemplations. But if she had to be lively in her delivery in order to persuade Aunt Fern to eat, then she would do so.

"It's only been today that I've not eaten. Surely I won't succumb to an early death quite so soon." Aunt Fern pursed her lips. "You know it's unbecoming of you two to conspire against me."

Aunt Myrtle put a ham sandwich in front of her sister. "But ally ourselves together, we must. If you'll recall, dear sister, you and Lydie did the very same thing to me that time at the county fair."

Lydie and Aunt Fern shared a knowing glance. Aunt Myrtle was gifted in many ways, but her attention to detail, especially when it came to baking, left much to be desired. The judges at the fair thought so as well when they tasted the sugarless blueberry pie Aunt Myrtle entered.

"True," said Aunt Fern. "But that was because that blueberry pie *was* awful. Who forgets to add sugar to a recipe?" She puckered her lips in a sour expression as if tasting the tart pie all over again. Unfortunately, they'd eaten far too much of it since there had been plenty of the pie left over after the judging.

Aunt Myrtle's brows perched low into a frown. "Bringing up the past is not conducive to this discussion."

"Alas, we shan't talk about that wretched blueberry pie when this is a difficult time in my life." Aunt Fern sniffled and daintily blew her nose in, thankfully, the handkerchief and not the lace doily.

Perhaps a licorice whip would ease some of Aunt Fern's melancholy. Lydie did have a penny saved up for a special purpose. After the noonday meal, she'd walk to the mercantile and purchase one of her aunt's favorite candies. And while she was there, Lydie would inquire as to whether there was a job opening for one or both of her aunts at the mercantile.

If that didn't work, she'd invite them both to follow her to Willow Falls.

If she accepted the position.

CHAPTER TWO

SOLOMON ELIASON SAT BEHIND the worn walnut desk in the Willow Falls church. A small area had been carved out from the rest of the church and boasted the desk, a slatted wooden chair, and an oil lamp. His Bible rested next to a few sheets of paper and a wood-and-graphite pencil. He steepled his fingers and pondered the words of his sermon—the first sermon he'd ever preach. It would be about forgiveness, a matter close to his heart and one he had personally struggled with over the years.

Would the townsfolk accept him as their new reverend? He'd received some kindly welcomes, including invitations to supper for the past few nights he'd been here, but he'd also heard mutterings from the time he'd arrived. Murmurings about how young he was and that he couldn't possibly have enough experience to preach.

True. He was only twenty-one and hadn't the experience of an older, more mature pastor. But he had a heart for sharing the Gospel, for caring for and serving others, and most importantly, he felt this was the Lord's calling on his life.

Even if Grandfather would argue otherwise.

Some had expressed concerns about the fact that he was unmarried. He hoped someday to marry, but for now, his job duties kept him far too busy to entertain courtship. Especially since he would be traveling once a month to nearby Nelsonville to preach in the church there as an interim pastor. He also had taken on several odd jobs to help supplement the meager earnings he would receive as a reverend.

Already, he'd been nominated to be on the school board and be in charge of a prank the students aimed to play on the new teacher. Apparently, one of the school board members suggested that to ease the anxiety of starting a new school, the pupils would be allowed to have one day where they played innocent and harmless pranks on the unsuspecting teacher. Solomon thought of crochety Miss Schunk from his school days in northern Iowa. It would take more than just one day of innocuous pranks to ease the nerves of having her for a teacher.

He chuckled to himself. While he'd endeavored to be an up-standing student, there had been a time or two when he engaged in some harmless pranks. Fortunately for the Willow Falls teacher, the pranks were only allowed on one day. For Miss Schunk, they were a common occurrence. Her face flashed in his mind. With piercing eyes, the woman rarely blinked. She had no time for shenanigans and even less time for laughter. It was no surprise to him she never married.

Pa had taken him aside and asked that he be a leader and convince the other students such pranks needed to cease. Solomon had shilly-shallied about it, but in the end, he obeyed Pa and did his best to be a respectable young man.

Pa. He missed him more than he let on, both he and Ma. They passed away from the influenza when Solomon was ten. Right at the time when he needed a godly role model to show him how to be the man God called him to be.

Instead, the remainder of his upbringing was provided by a harsh grandfather.

Solomon shoved the thoughts aside. When and if he did some-day marry, he hoped it would be someone like Ma and he endeavored to be someone like Pa. But until then, he would do his due diligence to preach the Word and make a difference, no matter how small, in the town of Willow Falls in the wild and ruthless Wyoming Territory.

Solomon could see the boardwalk from his location at the desk. Passersby greeted one another and he longed to be a part of this community he hoped to call home.

The sermon wasn't going to write itself, that much Solomon knew. Perhaps the forgiveness sermon would come at a later time. Maybe his first one should be on a less personal topic.

He tapped his pencil on the desk. With paper so expensive and not to be wasted, he best be sure of what he wished to write about before he penned it. Someday Solomon hoped to be a reverend who memorized his sermons, but for now, he needed nothing less than an outline.

Or maybe he should procrastinate. Thoughts of the new school teacher set to arrive in a few days again filled his mind. Apparently, the elderly spinster had been the only one who responded to the announcement. When the other four board members decided to open a school for the growing town of Willow Falls, they received no responses from their town, so they mailed advertisements to nearby Wyoming Territory towns, none of which Solomon had ever visited, including Nelsonville and Prune Creek.

According to Mr. Morton, there were no responses for some time. It would appear the eleven pupils would not have a teacher. Until what Mr. Morton surmised as a spinster woman, long in the tooth and with meticulous handwriting, wrote to express her interest.

For the children's sakes, Solomon hoped the teacher was nothing like Miss Schunk.

All the way to the mercantile, Lydie mentally tossed about the benefits and the disadvantages to accepting the teaching position. The favor was resting on accepting, but only slightly. And only if she could be sure her aunts would be provided for.

Lydie stepped inside and perused the items. While the sparse offerings could hardly be compared to those offered in Minnesota, there were some splendid wares hidden amongst the foodstuffs, coffee, sewing notions, boots, elixirs, and the lone pine casket leaning against the wall. There were a few calico bonnets, some lovely pink and green ribbons, and an exquisite maroon-colored dress with a lace collar.

The latter captured her attention for a lengthy amount of time. She ran her fingers along the fabric and dreamed of owning such a splendid piece of clothing.

Her attention was then drawn to a wanted poster on the wall near the guns and bullets. It included a sketch of a frightening-looking man with dark eyes, a wide nose, and a scraggly beard. It offered a reward of $200 for the criminal who was wanted for killing someone at a saloon in the southern part of the Wyoming Territory. Lydie cringed. If the aunts knew outlaws like the man in the poster were on the loose, they'd never allow her to venture to another town.

Two other folks were in the store near the tools and harnesses. Lydie didn't mean to eavesdrop, but well, they *were* talking rather loudly.

"But we must find a caregiver for Mother and Father. Someone who will be even-tempered, patient, and merciful." The woman, wearing a dress that made the maroon one look drab, spoke in worried tones to a man beside her.

"Yes, my dear, and we shall. They have given us their blessing for our move to Massachusetts. You know they are welcome to move there with us, but cannot due to their failing health." The man, dressed in a black, woolen, double-breasted frock coat, reached for the woman's hands. "My dear, do not fret. There must be someone who can care for your parents while we handle business back East."

"But how can you be so certain?"

"God has always provided."

The woman wrung her hands. "But I shall miss them."

"Yes, and I as well. But remember, we will be back in a few weeks for a visit and then again next summer." He paused and Lydie watched him lean toward the woman and plant a kiss on her cheek. "And we will visit as often as you'd like. If that is a couple times a year when the weather is acceptable, then a couple times a year it shall be."

"You are my husband and I want to go with you to Massachusetts, but this is just such a quandary."

Lydie had no idea who this couple was or who the woman's parents were. Still new to the area, she knew only a handful of residents. Their clothing suggested they were not typical townsfolk.

"Now, pick a trinket and put your mind at ease about your parents," the man suggested, gesturing to a shelf of fine China, a music box, and a porcelain doll.

Suddenly a thought occurred to Lydie. What if *she* knew someone, or two someones, who might be the answer to the couple's dilemma? Dare she utter her thoughts?

Lord, shall I?

She chewed on her lip and watched as the woman chose an ornate wooden music box with a painted butterfly on the top. Lydie prayed again and then prayed once more.

Gathering her courage to speak to strangers, Lydie walked toward the couple. "Excuse me, ma'am and sir." Her mouth grew dry and she willed her nerves to settle.

"Yes?" the woman's red eyes indicated she'd been crying.

"I wasn't eavesdropping." Lydie paused, wishing she could forsake her shyness just this once. "All right, perhaps I was eavesdropping, but I may have a solution to your predicament."

The woman's eyes enlarged and the man leaned closer. "That would be an answer to prayer if you do," the woman said.

"You see, I have two aunts, Fern and Myrtle. They are wonderful godly women who are kind, gracious, patient, long-suffering, and the like. Perhaps they might be just who you are looking for to care for your elderly parents."

According to the mantle clock displayed on the shelf, it took only seven minutes to convince the couple that the aunts were perfect for the position.

CHAPTER THREE

LYDIE GRABBED THE BROOM. If she hurried, she could have the cabin completely cleaned before the aunts arrived back from their first meeting with the Peabodys. She wanted to surprise them.

And she needed something to keep her mind off the disquieting reality that she would soon be leaving her family.

Lydie swept the dirt into a pile, removed it from the cabin, and bustled about putting away the sparse collection of clean dishes. Would she embrace her new job in Willow Falls? Would the pupils like her? Would she like the town? Would she be able to manage without seeing Aunt Myrtle and Aunt Fern every day? Lydie would miss their sisterly camaraderie and even their bickering-filled disputes.

Perhaps she should stay and see if she could help with the caregiving at the Peabody house until such time as Miss Owsten no longer taught school in Prune Creek.

Lydie was about to start on the washing when the aunts came bustling through the door. She could always discern when they were scheming something, and today was no exception. Aunt Fern was the worst when it came to being subtle. Her eyes always darted about when she was suspicious, and it made Lydie wonder if they had been able to keep their mischievous ways a secret from their ma. Aunt Fern shuffled and rattled something behind her back.

"There you are," said Aunt Myrtle, as if Lydie had somehow thought to disappear then decided against it. She tossed a mischievous glance toward her sister. "Shall we?"

"We shall."

Aunt Myrtle patted Lydie on the arm. "Do have a seat, child. We need to speak with you posthaste."

The last time they needed to speak with her "posthaste" was when the aunts decided they were moving to the Wyoming Territory so Aunt Fern could marry the man she met through correspondence. Surely this would not be quite as life-altering.

She took a seat at the table. Aunt Myrtle smirked. Aunt Fern again rustled whatever was behind her back.

"As you know," Aunt Myrtle, always the spokeswoman of the two, began. "Aunt Fern and I secured the position as caregivers for the Peabodys. Were it not for your astuteness while in the mercantile, we would never have procured this position."

Aunt Myrtle had a way of drawing things out into lengthy lectures while Aunt Fern stood by and nodded in agreement. Or spoke out in disagreement.

"You'll be leaving for Willow Falls in a few days. There, you'll be starting a new life as a teacher."

Aunt Fern sniffled.

"As such," continued Aunt Myrtle, "Fern and I have two gifts we would like to bestow upon you in celebration of this new chapter in your life."

"I don't have to leave. I could stay here and work with you at the Peabody home. Perhaps I could do the laundering or maybe push Mr. Peabody around in his wheelchair or..."

Aunt Myrtle shook her head. "No, child. Those are benevolent suggestions and Fern and I appreciate your offer, but we are proud of the fact that you are going to be a teacher. You have a gift and a way with others. You're soft-spoken, sweet, and thoughtful. You care for others and are a smart and godly young woman."

"Yes," added Aunt Fern. "We have long prayed for God to guide you in His plan for your life. Perhaps this is that answer to prayer."

Lydie swallowed the lump that had formed in her throat. If she couldn't bear *thinking* about leaving these precious aunts, how could she ever actually *do* it? And while the aunts *pretended* to put on a facade, Lydie knew them well enough to know they would struggle with this change as much as she would.

"And now for the gifts. The first is that we shall accompany you to Willow Falls to safely deposit you there. We went to the stage stop today after visiting with the Peabodys and secured three tickets. We will be your chaperones and will ensure this Willow Falls town is suitable for our niece. Should we arrive and find it to be contemptible with gunfights in the streets, skirmishes with Indians, and the like..." Aunt Myrtle squared her shoulders. "We shall bring you back without delay."

The thought of gunfights in the streets or skirmishes with Indians had crossed Lydie's mind about four hundred times. The knowledge of the aunts chaperoning her to the town and bringing her back to Prune Creek should anything be amiss comforted her greatly. "Thank you, Aunt Myrtle and Aunt Fern. I am so appreciative that you are coming with me."

"Yes, well, it's better than waiting to see if there is some elderly woman or a kindly couple that would be willing to chaperone you. Besides, we haven't had an adventure in a while."

"Not since we decided to answer the letter of that deceptive cad," quipped Aunt Fern.

Lydie jumped up to embrace the aunts, but Aunt Myrtle shook her head. "There will be time for hugs in a moment. First, we have one other gift for you." She nodded toward her sister.

"Close your eyes and hold out your hands," directed Aunt Fern.

Lydie did as she was told and placed her hands palms up, the anticipation nearly more than she could stand. Aunt Fern placed a somewhat heavy, but soft item seemingly made of paper in her hands. A parcel, perhaps?

"Open your eyes," the aunts chorused.

She gazed at the gift wrapped in brown paper.

"Do open it," suggested Aunt Fern.

Lydie removed the ribbon and pulled away the paper to reveal...

She gasped. In her hands was the maroon-colored dress she'd seen at the mercantile. Giddiness overwhelmed her, and with a shaky hand, she unfolded the dress and held it up. The rich and vibrant fabric was smooth and velvety in her hands. She laid it across her lap and ran her fingers over it. An ornate lace collar embellished the neckline and white puffy sleeves near the wrists added to its elegant appearance.

Had she ever seen anything so opulent?

"Oh, Aunt Myrtle and Aunt Fern..." Her heart sang with delight. "How were you able to afford such an exquisite dress?" Such luxuries were far beyond anything they could afford.

"Never you mind about that," said Aunt Myrtle. "I had some funds saved for an important expenditure and Aunt Fern here had something she needed to rid herself of in exchange for a few pennies."

The necklace from Mr. Wilkins. Lydie had seen it when it arrived in the mail one day in Minnesota. A trinket declaring the man's love for her aunt and used to persuade her to move to the Wyoming Territory. "But, Aunt Fern, you could have used the money from the necklace for something else. For necessities rather than this lavish dress."

Aunt Fern's eyebrow quirked. "I could have, but I didn't."

"And you, Aunt Myrtle, you have so little money saved. Surely it could have been put to better use."

"Can't see how," declared her aunt.

Tears in her eyes, Lydie placed the dress on the table and embraced her aunts. They'd always been there for her since the time she was three-years-old. Always loving, caring for, and making sure she knew she was loved. And now this incredible sacrifice.

"We wanted you to have something beautiful to start your new position as a teacher. This is a momentous occasion. A special celebration for you as you take this next step in your life." Aunt Fern's eyes misted.

Aunt Myrtle held the dress up to Lydie. "You're such a petite thing, but I think I can take it in and give it a good hemming before we leave."

"She'll do a fine job altering the dress, but don't let her bake you any goodies for the journey," chortled Aunt Fern. She and Lydie exchanged a knowing glance. Aunt Myrtle was a gifted seamstress, but a baker she was not.

"Now, now." Aunt Myrtle placed her hands on her ample hips. "I'll have none of that. You know as well as I do that my baking is just as good as yours."

Aunt Fern pressed her lips together in a straight line. "Pfft."

And as Lydie stood watching her aunts bicker about whether or not Aunt Myrtle should be allowed to bake goodies, a tear slid down her face.

Lord, help me as I embark on this new adventure, for I shall miss them so.

CHAPTER FOUR

SOLOMON UNFOLDED THE LETTER he'd received from Grandfather right before he embarked on a life of new beginnings.

Solomon,

By the time you receive this, you'll be heading off to the Wyoming Territory. You know I strongly disagree with your choices and I've made my opinions known about my disappointment in you. You'd do well to stay in Minnesota and work on the farm rather than chase some futile dream. Your ma chased her fanciful dream and married a man I disapproved of. Then she moved to Iowa. Neither was a wise choice.

I could insist you stay in Minnesota rather than become a ne'er-do-well without a promising future. I could demand you give careful thought to the kind of life you'll lead in a place full of outlaws as you'll likely become one of them. But you wouldn't listen. You're like your ma that way. Always going her own way and never heeding wise counsel. Look where it got her. Married to a Scotsman without a penny to his name.

I regret to inform you that if you make this ill-advised decision, you'll no longer be welcome here neither as my grandson nor as a guest.

Grandfather

Solomon stared at the letter. Grandfather had never been proud of him. Never thought he made the right choices and never supported him in any of his endeavors. Solomon knew he hadn't supported Ma's choice to marry a poor immigrant from Scotland and had done all he could to keep them apart. He recalled Ma's tearful words about how difficult Grandfather could be and that he lacked compassion. But Ma hadn't told him these things so he would dislike the man he would eventually be raised by, but so that Solomon could join her and Pa in prayer for Grandfather. And so that Solomon would understand why Grandfather never came to visit.

When Ma married Pa, he no longer wished to see his daughter. Now the same was happening to Solomon.

While Ma never spoke of her growing up years, Solomon surmised it hadn't been easy being reared by a bitter man who demanded things always be his way.

It was the orphanage or live with Grandfather, and while no love was offered, Solomon did have a place to live until he developed the courage to venture out on his own. Grandfather made it clear that he was only allowed to live there provided he earned his keep. That he was merely another hired hand with high expectations to work hard and never complain.

But Solomon's hard work on the farm was never enough.

He tasted the sour bitterness. No, he ought not preach on forgiveness just yet. Not until his heart was right with God on the matter.

Solomon finished his sermon on serving others and tucked it into his Bible. Tomorrow he'd preach his first sermon. If all else failed and the residents of Willow Falls found him lacking as Grandfather always had, he could become a circuit rider.

Maybe avoiding staying in one place would guard against others so easily witnessing his failures.

The day arrived for Lydie to move to Willow Falls. She and the aunts, along with several other passengers, stood before the red stagecoach with yellow wheels. The driver, a giant of a man with a thick and bushy blond beard, addressed them in a stern voice. "Let it be known there are some rules to riding on this here stagecoach."

Lydie had heard the rules before when she, Aunt Myrtle, and Aunt Fern traveled from Minnesota to the Wyoming Territory. Still, she offered her rapt attention to the surly man.

"If you don't wanna ride, you can always get off at any time, but it's a long way back." One of the men in the group chuckled, but the driver did not share his amusement. He narrowed his eyes at the man before he continued. "There are hungry coyotes, wolves, and the like, so it'd be in your best interests not to wander off if we have any runaway horses."

A woman gasped and raised her hand slightly. "But, sir, you don't anticipate runaway horses, do you?"

"Can't say." The driver spit to the side, narrowly missing one of the other passengers' shoes. "Men, there will be no coarse language around the womenfolk. No smoking in the stagecoach. Save your cigars for when we stop at a station. Don't be shooting out the window all willy-nilly at the animals in hopes of elk stew for supper. The sound of gunfire could upset the horses, and then they'd run real fast and maybe even crash over the side of the mountain."

Aunt Myrtle held a hand to her bosom. "Has that ever happened?"

"Yep, couple of times. The worst was back in '67 when the stagecoach overturned from going too fast and crushed a man's arm. Wasn't a pleasant thing to see. Then there were some hostile Indians in the area and...let's just say don't be shooting out the window." He cleared his throat. "Lastly, no snoring if you fall asleep, and don't be asking when we'll get to the next station because ain't no one gonna tell you, so don't be a clodpoll and ask a dozen times. Any questions?"

A rotund man asked if there was sufficient food at the stations. Another asked if he could chew his tobacco, to which the driver answered, "Sure. If you're by a window. And spit with the wind when you do spit."

Moments later, they climbed aboard, with Aunt Fern reassuring a nervous woman that it was just a short ride over the mountain and that if she wanted a real adventure, try traveling all the way from Minnesota.

The stagecoach wound around winding curves and through the mountains from Prune Creek to Willow Falls. It was enough to cause Lydie's breakfast to resurface. She sat wedged between the aunts in an overly-full coach as it jostled to and fro. The roads were rutted at best and impassable at worst. Twice the men had to help push the stagecoach when it became stuck.

Lydie struggled to keep her eyes open but only once nodded completely off, resting her head on Aunt Fern's shoulder. A loud and brash woman on board reminded Lydie it was in poor taste to rest her head on anyone's shoulder, related or not. From that moment on, she did her best to sleep only when she could manage sitting straight up.

When they finally reached Willow Falls late that evening, Lydie deemed herself unlikely to ever ride on such transportation again.

After a night's rest at a room in the mercantile, the only place available since there was no hotel in Willow Falls, Lydie bid her aunts goodbye. "I think it best to board the stagecoach and return with you posthaste to Prune Creek," she said, sniffling.

"But this is where you belong, even if it's only for a season." Aunt Fern brushed wispy strands of hair from Lydie's face and planted a kiss on her forehead. "You will come to visit Aunt Myrtle and me with a chaperone, of course, and we will pay you a visit as well. And there will be plenty of letters to write."

Lydie saw the emotion just below the surface in both of her aunts' expressions. She would miss them dearly. "If I discover this teaching position is not for me, will you come retrieve me?"

"We absolutely will," confirmed Aunt Myrtle. She placed an arm around Lydie's shoulders. "We dreaded this day would come when you would forge your own path in life. But we are so proud of you."

"Proud of you indeed," agreed Aunt Fern. "We love you and are only a short trip away over the mountain."

The tears fell swiftly as the aunts boarded the stagecoach. It wasn't too late to change her mind. To return home with Aunt Myrtle and Aunt Fern. To forego the teaching position.

Lydie wasn't sure she wanted to face this new chapter in her life.

Chapter Five

TWO DAYS LATER, AFTER meeting with Mr. Morton and discovering she was to stay with the Castleberrys, a prominent couple, for her room and board, Lydie was ready to begin teaching.

As ready as she could be.

She pinned her mother's cameo brooch on the collar of the maroon dress. She'd wear the dress today and henceforth wear it only for church and special occasions, but the aunts had insisted she wear it her first day teaching. In Aunt Myrtle's words, the color of the dress contrasted beautifully with her dark hair. In Aunt Fern's words, there had never been a lovelier young lady.

"Best let us know if any potential suitors who are not suitable attempt to court you," she declared.

Lydie wasn't concerned. While many women her age were ready for marriage before the tender age of nineteen, she would wait until the perfect man came along. She'd not give her heart to a cad like Mr. Wilkins.

She entered the school well before the students were to arrive. A humble building, it was a quarter of the size of her school in Minnesota. Before long, the wood stove in the corner would be put to good use due to the cold winters she'd heard the Wyoming Territory was known for.

She shivered at the thought. What would she do when it was too cold and snowy to either travel to see the aunts or have them travel to see her?

Lydie attempted to push aside the homesickness that lingered from the day she'd arrived. She wanted to make Aunt Myrtle and Aunt Fern proud of her, but if things didn't work out, she'd send a letter and make good on the aunts' promise to retrieve her immediately.

But oh, how she wanted this position to be like what she'd dreamed it could be. Lydie ran a hand along the top of the desk and sat in the chair. "Now, students, please turn to page fifteen in your primers," she practiced, her voice echoing throughout the building. "Do remember to practice your spelling words for our upcoming spelling bee." She again pretended to address her pupils. "Please, students, do prepare for recitation. After that, we will sing two songs, first *The Star-Spangled Banner*, followed by *Old Folks at Home*. Let's now practice the former."

And on it went, until she rehearsed every line she anticipated saying. She even practiced scolding a wayward pupil by having him write on the chalkboard one hundred times in his best penmanship, "I will not steal Bertha's slate." She spoke louder and was bolder than her usual shy self.

Finally, she stood and walked back and forth across the front of the room while telling her pupils a story that would assist them in learning their history lesson.

All would be well.

It had to be.

Solomon strolled along the boardwalk waiting for the mercantile to open so he could purchase more paper. He anticipated his sermon on honesty would be lengthier than he originally anticipated.

The door of the schoolhouse was open as if to beckon the students. He hadn't yet met the new elderly spinster teacher, but as the reverend and a member of the school board, he should make it a priority. Perhaps after school he would stop in and introduce himself.

A loud, exaggerated voice rang from the schoolhouse, and in curiosity, he edged closer.

"Now students, please turn to page fifteen in your primers." The voice paused. "Do remember to practice your spelling words for our upcoming spelling bee."

Solomon was now near the window. He peered through it only to see what appeared to be a student whom he didn't recognize.

"Please, students, do prepare for recitation. After that, we will sing two songs, first *The Star-Spangled Banner* followed by *Old Folks at Home.*" The student began to sing while waving her arms about as if holding a baton. He'd seen a music conductor once years ago when an orchestra practiced in the city. Did she believe herself to be a conductor?

O! say, can you see, by the dawn's early light,
What so proudly we hailed at the twilight's last gleaming:
Whose broad stripes and bright stars through the perilous fight,
O'er the ramparts we watched were so gallantly streaming,

And the rocket's red glare, the bombs bursting in air,
Gave proof through the night that our flag was still there;

She paused then, and changed her voice from a singing voice to a louder one chastising a fellow student. "Now, George, that was not acceptable behavior. Do return the slate to Bertha."

He squinted to see who she was talking to, but there was no one else in the schoolhouse. With a swish of her skirts, the pupil turned quickly. "George, I want you to write 'I will not steal Bertha's slate' on the chalkboard in your best penmanship one hundred times." She pretended to hand a piece of chalk to another student.

Solomon had heard of a new family who moved to town last week, but he'd yet to meet them. Mrs. Morton mentioned they had a daughter and two sons. Perhaps this was the daughter. Poor soul must have arrived at school long before the others and was bored. He leaned back from the window just as more students arrived.

Today was the first day of school and the only day for the pranks. How would the teacher, whom he imagined looked like Miss Schunk, handle it? Was he supposed to monitor their actions?

A thought suddenly hit him like a runaway horse galloping down the street at full speed. He was to have met with the pupils before class and give them proper instructions and reminders. He was to reiterate to them the pranks were only for today and that they should cease with the pranks if things got unruly and disorderly.

Maybe Solomon could still catch some of the students before they entered the classroom.

But as he was about to make good on his decision, the last student in a line of them entered the schoolhouse.

The first pupils entered the schoolhouse a few minutes later. Lydie attempted to calm her racing heart. *Lord, please help me*, she pleaded.

She introduced herself, asked the children to introduce themselves, led the children in the Pledge of Allegiance, and began to discuss their first assignment when the most awful thing happened. Each of the eleven students rested their heads on their desks and went to sleep.

"Students," she squeaked, bemoaning once again that she was soft-spoken.

No one paid her any mind.

Lydie walked between the row of desks. One child was snoring and another's eyelids fluttered. She hadn't even begun her lesson. Was her teaching method so utterly boring that they could not stay awake?

Her eyes stung. She wanted so badly to succeed at this endeavor. To make the aunts proud. To resist the temptation to send a letter asking them to retrieve her because she already missed them so.

"Students, if you would…" but once again, they ignored her or didn't hear her because sleep had overcome them. Perhaps they weren't feeling well. Once when she was a youngster, nearly everyone in school had a minor illness preventing them from attending school for two days. Should she send the pupils home? Start school tomorrow?

Lydie waited a while longer and again flipped through the pages of the primer and organized the two extra slates on her desk. She erased any extra smudge marks on the chalkboard, although she'd already done that twice.

Once she thought she saw one of the young boys open an eye briefly and she started toward his desk. But when she arrived, he had fallen asleep once again.

How could it be that she was so awake and ready to face the day, but her young charges were languid and lethargic?

Lydie prayed and then prayed some more for wisdom.

Finally, after what seemed like an eternity, the pupils arose from their slumber and suddenly became energetic hooligans. A group of three girls started singing *The Star-Spangled Banner*, two other girls broke out in tune to *It Came Upon a Midnight Clear*, and one girl was singing an off-key version of *Mary Had a Little Lamb*. Two boys began chatting nonstop about which creeks had the best fishing, two other boys sat on the floor and played jacks. One boy of about ten-years-old tapped his pencil on his desk while eyeing her with a rebellious stare.

"Everyone, if you could direct your attention to the front of the room." But no one paid her any mind. She glanced out the window and eyed the church across the street. Maybe a seasoned preacher would have wise words of counsel. Perhaps he could give a sermon on the importance of obeying authority. It wouldn't take long to march over to the parsonage, providing he was there, and ask him for assistance. As a man of the cloth, he would be bound to confidentiality, whereas someone she might seek help from at the mercantile or post office might not be.

Lydie cringed at the thought of everyone in town knowing of her predicament. And if the school board found out, would they relieve her of her duties? Yes, seeking the reverend's assistance was the only feasible answer.

Clutching her skirts, Lydie rushed out the door, down the steps, and toward the church. If he wasn't in the church, the preacher should be in the parsonage. Would he mind a distressed future congregant pounding on his door at this hour?

Lydie Marie Beauchamp, you mustn't fail.

The town was lively with folks meandering up and down the boardwalk. Horses neighed and the aroma of flowers from a flower patch near the church floated on the air.

But Lydie paid all of that no mind. She had a mission and the sooner she was able to teach, the better. She meandered through the church to a room at the right of the sanctuary. The door stood slightly ajar and she knocked gently, while simultaneously attempting to fight the tears that threatened.

CHAPTER SIX

SOLOMON SAT AT HIS desk attempting to write on the subject of honesty. He flipped through the pages of his well-read Bible. He must deliver a captivating sermon and prove he was the one for this position. Something that would impress the elders and the residents of Willow Falls. He was finding they were not an easy lot to convince.

He reclined back in the uncomfortable chair and laced his fingers behind his head. When he'd envisioned doing the Lord's work, he hadn't imagined it would be so difficult. After all, hadn't he practiced numerous times addressing his future congregants? Hadn't he spent a lengthy time in prayer? Studied the Bible from front to back?

Solomon wrote a few sentences on the paper, then erased them. He leaned forward and rested his head in his hands. He wanted to succeed. To prove to Grandfather he'd made the correct choice in vocation. To prove he was worthy of the calling God placed on his life.

"Sir?"

He glanced up from his frustrated stupor to see a woman standing before him. She looked vaguely familiar. "Yes?"

"Sir, might you know where I could find the reverend? It's of utmost importance I locate him immediately."

He strained to hear her timid voice. "The reverend?"

"Yes. Might you know where he is?" The young woman peered from left to right and out the door leading to the sanctuary.

And that's when he realized why she looked familiar. Solomon chuckled. He'd seen her at the school talking to herself and pacing and figured she was a student. But upon closer examination, he could see she was no pupil. Slight in stature, but her face was that of a young woman close to his own age.

A lovely young woman.

Solomon blinked and averted his gaze to the blank sheet of paper on his desk.

"Sir?" Her tone indicated desperation.

He cleared his throat. "I am the reverend, miss."

"With all respect, might there be a seasoned man of the cloth here?"

Solomon did his best to quell his irritation. Just because he was young did not mean he was inept. Pride threatened to rear its head and, with some difficulty, he tamped it down. "I am the only reverend. How might I be of assistance?"

"Oh, my sincerest apologies." Her face matched the color of her dress. "I need help."

Finally. Someone he could assist. Someone whose life he could make a difference in. Should they open with prayer? He rifled through memorized Bible verses that might be of aid to her. Psalm 46:1? The entirety of Psalm 91? Philippians 4:6-7?

"Sir? Reverend?"

Her despair drew him back to the task at hand. "I'm happy to help you, ma'am."

"Please come to the school and preach a sermon about respecting authority to those wayward pupils." She wrung her hands and distress shone on her pretty face.

"Wayward pupils?"

"Yes. First they slept and now they're rambunctious. And they are paying me no mind. Whatever shall I do?"

It hit him like a wagon full of goods. This woman, whom he once thought was a student, was the new teacher. She was not an elderly spinster. Far from it. She was not like Miss Schunk. Quite the opposite.

He swallowed hard. The reason for her predicament was because of the prank. And he was to have spoken to the students on their way to school and remind them about the rules. Yet, he'd forgotten.

"I can help you." He stood. "I'm Reverend Solomon Eliason."

"Miss Lydie Beauchamp. Might we go? I'm fearful of what they may do next." It appeared she might say something more, but instead Miss Beauchamp turned and rushed from the church.

For a petite woman she could walk fast, and Solomon hastened his strides to keep up with her. He could hear the voices even before they reached the schoolhouse. Several someones were singing off-key and he resisted the urge to cover his ears.

"Do you see what I mean?" Miss Beauchamp asked when they entered.

Oh, he could see it all right. Solomon viewed the antics of the boisterous children and dreaded the repercussions. One little boy ran up to him. "Are we doing it right, Reverend? The noise and all?"

From his peripheral, he noticed an alarmed expression overcome Miss Beauchamp's countenance.

One of the off-key singers skipped to where he stood. "How long shall we continue this, Reverend? You forgot to tell us if it was for the entire day or just for the morning."

Solomon cringed. This was all his fault. Miss Beauchamp's eyes bored into him and he prayed for courage as he faced her.

With narrowed eyes and hands on her hips, she spoke. "You knew about this?"

"I...uh...I did."

"And you condone such behavior?"

"I...uh...don't."

"Might you tell me what is the meaning of this?"

She might be small and unassuming, but at this moment, the diminutive woman was full of spunk.

"I...Miss Beauchamp...I can explain."

"Do you like our singing?" a girl asked.

Another boy sidled up to Solomon. "This is the best day of school ever. Thanks for giving us permission to be naughty."

The teacher pursed her lips. "And you were saying you can explain?" This time Miss Beauchamp's words came out as more of the seething variety.

"Students, I'm Reverend Solomon." The room hushed immediately and he had the children's attention.

He was aware of Miss Beauchamp's stare directed toward him. Or was it a glower?

"The prank is now over. Thank you for participating."

He heard her sharp intake of breath and immediately regretted his choice of words.

"Uh...yes, so now do heed the words of the Lord when He admonishes us to respect and obey authority." He reiterated a few more Scripture verses to support his lecture before continuing. "Now that the prank has concluded, please refrain from playing any more tricks on Miss Beauchamp. Does everyone understand?"

A hand waved in the air from a boy Solomon didn't recognize. "Yes?"

"But I thought this was for all day. Why are we stopping early?"

Miss Beauchamp had pressed her mouth into a straight line and her eyes seemed to bulge. It was clear as the beak on a chicken that she was furious with him, and he put some additional distance between them. "We are stopping early and the pranks will now cease. "

Several murmured "Yes, sirs" followed and Reverend Solomon straightened his posture. He whispered to Miss Beauchamp, "There. All fixed."

She, however, was far less enthusiastic than he was at his achievement. He offered her a weak smile.

A smile she did not return. Clearly she was not amused. Miffed even.

There was only one way to rectify the situation, and even then...

Grandfather's words played in his mind. He'd once forgotten to shut the barn door. It was right after his parents died and he was sent to live with Grandfather. Distraught and overwhelmed by the loss of the two people he loved most, Solomon had done his chores as directed, but failed to heed Grandfather's directive about the door. *"Only a fool or a simpleton would leave the door open."*

Grandfather hadn't spoken to him for two days after his error, and after that for some time, only begrudgingly and not without bringing up the incident. He'd never offered forgiveness for Solomon's error.

Likely only a fool or a simpleton would forget to tell the students the parameters of the prank.

The remainder of the school day went fairly smoothly. But while the day was going better, Lydie wasn't ready to give accolades to Reverend Solomon for such a feat. Apparently, he was behind the shenanigans.

What a brash and insolent cad!

She immediately regretted her thoughts toward a man of the cloth. But still...he had been instrumental in allowing the pupils to exhibit disrespect and in some way, unbeknownst to her, attributed to their unruliness.

That evening, tucked in the comfortable room at the Castleberrys' spacious home, Lydie put pencil to paper and wrote a letter to the aunts.

Dearest Aunt Myrtle and Aunt Fern,

You won't believe my first day as a teacher. The words "horrific," "distressing," and "alarming" come to mind. Unbeknownst to me that it was a prank, the pupils proceeded to pretend to go to sleep on their desks and then, in a rapid turnabout of circumstances, became spirited and lively. Some were singing, others were playing, and still others were participating in rambunctious behavior. They listened to not a word I said. Dismayed at the entire situation—the term "at my wit's end" comes to mind—I left the schoolhouse in search of the reverend as the church is near the school.

I expected an elderly gent with experience in handling wayward children. Instead, Reverend Solomon Eliason is a young man not much older than myself. While this is difficult to fathom, he was the one who instigated the entire event. He is a rather disagreeable fellow. While I laugh at it now, the irony of his name being "Solomon" did not strike me as humorous at the time.

Needless to say, I barely survived the ordeal. After the reverend quieted the children, the day was without incident, for which I am grateful.

Other than the prank and Reverend Solomon's involvement, I believe I will like it here. Willow Falls is a friendly town and the Castleberrys, whom I am boarding with, are a kindly couple. I've never stayed in a room so spacious and ornately decorated.

Aunt Fern, I do hope you are doing much better after the melancholy you experienced at the hands of Mr. Wilkins. Are you and Aunt Myrtle settling into your position as caretakers for the Peabodys?

I would be remiss if I didn't mention that I am homesick. I miss you both so much and wish you could have moved here with me.

Lydie paused and held her pencil midair. She could imagine the worry lines increasing on the aunts' faces when they read her last two lines. She didn't want them to worry. Thank goodness she hadn't mentioned just how homesick she was.

Please do not fret as I am fine and hope to see you both before Christmas.

Much love,

Lydie

She folded the letter and placed it in the envelope to mail tomorrow.

Lydie thought again about Reverend Solomon. Oh, he was a dapper man to be sure with those broad shoulders, hazel eyes, and light brown hair. But a gentleman he was not.

CHAPTER SEVEN

THE FOLLOWING DAY AFTER Lydie mailed the letter to the aunts, she walked to the mercantile for some thread. She was relieved to discover the students did not engage in any pranks today. No sleeping on their desks and no excitable and outlandish behavior. All in all, the day had been rather calm.

The thoughts about how a reverend could instigate such pranks were rarely far from her mind. Never would such behavior be accepted at the school she attended as a child.

But she'd not think about such things right now. No, at this moment, with the exception of missing Aunt Myrtle and Aunt Fern something awful, the day was near perfect.

Mr. Morton, the mercantile proprietor, swept the boardwalk in front of his shop. At first, Lydie was tempted to walk on past with only a slight, but respectful nod. But then she remembered that in order to overcome her shyness, she must actually speak.

"Hello," she greeted, her voice sounding somewhat hushed and timorous. "Hello, Mr. Morton," she repeated, her voice raising an octave.

"Good afternoon, Miss Beauchamp."

It was delightful how she was already beginning to know several people in the town. The aunts would be proud of her tenacity in attempting to overcome her timidity. *"Just take small steps and someday you'll be as gregarious as I am."* Aunt Myrtle's words echoed in her mind.

Her aunts. The thought of them jolted her once again. What were they doing right now? How were they taking to their positions caring for the Peabodys? How was Aunt Fern's broken heart? Had they made it back safely on that tumultuous stage-coach?

Lydie stepped inside the mercantile, focusing on the shelf with the fabric, needles, and thread. Perhaps some lovely hand-kerchiefs would make perfect gifts for the aunts for Christmas. She could embroider their initials on the front and stitch red edging around the perimeters. Lydie smoothed the pale-yellow fabric and began to formulate in her mind the outcome of the finished presents.

Her thoughts of sewing Christmas gifts were interrupted by a nearby conversation.

"You should have seen her face," a young voice, albeit familiar, said. "Her mouth was in the shape of the letter 'o'." The boy laughed. "We were supposed to be sleeping on our desks like you told us, Reverend, but I peeked just a little bit and that's when I saw her face. Reckon she was in a huff all right."

Lydie sucked in a breath. Had she just heard correctly? More details about that dreadful experience on her first day teaching? She peered around the corner. Reverend Solomon had the grace to avoid eye contact.

"We really bluffed our way, and it was all because of you," continued the boy she now recognized as Frederick Morton. "It was some mighty good plannin' on your part, Reverend, and the pranks were a nifty idea."

"Frederick..." began Reverend Solomon. He held a finger to his mouth as if to hush Frederick's nonstop flow of words.

But Frederick, whom Lydie suspected was a precocious lad, continued with his creative yarn. "And then Pa said it was only that one day that we got to play pranks. At first, I was disappointed."

Mr. Morton was in on the prank as well? How many other townsfolk knew of the tomfoolery? Lydie's breath hitched. Moisture slicked her palms and she discreetly wiped them on her dress in the guise of pressing out imaginary wrinkles.

Thankfully, there was no one else in the mercantile besides her, Frederick, and Reverend Solomon.

"Frederick, we do need to discuss some things about this. As you know..." But Reverend Solomon stopped short when Frederick abruptly turned toward Lydie.

"Oh, hello, Miss Beauchamp. Didn't know you were standing there."

Lydie placed her hands on her hips and pursed her lips as she'd seen Aunt Fern do.

A low rumble of a chuckle sounded and a smile flashed across the reverend's face.

"Do you find all of this humorous, Reverend Solomon?"

"Uh, no, I don't. It's just that..." he released one more chuckle, then sobered. Lydie produced her sternest scowl, one that would make Aunt Myrtle proud.

Frederick inched a few steps backwards. "Reverend Solomon, she's giving you the same look Ma gives me when I sneak another cookie. I think you're in trouble."

Solomon hoped some of that irritation was directed toward Frederick as well. Miss Beauchamp's expression was indeed one of annoyance. Her hands placed firmly on her hips and her chin lifted high may have indicated her displeasure, but her petite stature did little to help her cause. He nearly chuckled at her bristling demeanor. It reminded him of a puppy who thought herself a wolf.

He really needed to explain to her the details of the pranks and how they'd gone awry. He hadn't slept well since the entire ordeal and the guilt piled on his shoulders like an oxen yoke. "Miss Beauchamp..." His mouth tasted like someone had placed a desert in it.

"Reverend Solomon, with all due respect, I believe I have heard enough. I'll just fetch the items I came here for and be on my way."

He didn't have to be the most astute individual to see that there was not only vexation in her expression, but also some hurt. The guilt piled on him all the more. "Ma'am, I do need to explain that it was my idea, but..."

"Exactly as I presumed."

"But, well, not my idea entirely, but..." His tongue was tied in a million knots and any logical words stuck in his throat. Instead, he sounded like a bumbling oaf. "I...you see...I meant...well, what I mean to say is that..."

Frederick raised his eyebrows. "I haven't never heard you talk like that before, Reverend. Do you have a speaking condition?"

Oh, he had a "speaking condition," all right. For one, it didn't help to have Frederick in the room. And two, the way Miss Beauchamp stood there, her eyes wide and her forehead puckered, all angry with him, but looking quite beautiful at the same time...

He shook his head. The lack of sleep had fiddled with his mind. Never before had he been at a loss for what needed to be said. He'd make a stuffed bird laugh with the way he was acting.

And then his inability to withhold the amusement that had escaped—amusement not only because of her expression, but also because he recalled her singing in the schoolhouse before he knew she was the teacher. Solomon chuckled again. Miss Beauchamp's animated chirpy voice would forever be ingrained in his mind, especially when she had addressed imaginary students.

Such an episode necessitated a letter to the aunts. How she wished she could sit around the table, eat one of Aunt Myrtle's bland sandwiches, and share with them about all that had transpired. How she wished she could hear their reassuring voices of comfort. Had they received her last letter, or was it stuck somewhere in the mountains between Willow Falls and Prune Creek?

Dearest Aunt Myrtle and Aunt Fern,
I am not at all sure I am meant to be a teacher. The prank was lamentable and I've already detailed the horrific events in a prior letter, but there is now more to add.

First of all, you would be proud of me. I have attempted to push aside my reserved nature and be a bit more boisterous. Not like you, Aunt Myrtle, but an improvement over my timid nature, to be sure. I have spoken to townsfolk on the street.

Lydie paused and tapped her pencil on the bureau. Just one person on the street so far, but still, that counted. And she would speak to others at church on Sunday if she wasn't "cowering" as Aunt Fern referred to it.

She continued to write her letter.

When I went to the mercantile, that brash Reverend Solomon was there. He did indeed plan the prank and seemed rather proud about it. He would not so much as offer an apology. It didn't help that Frederick Morton, a youngster at school, was sharing with him the details of my facial expressions while the pranks were being conducted.

Goodness, but what am I to think of such behavior?

I hope all is well in Prune Creek. Love and miss you both.

Lydie

CHAPTER EIGHT

SOLOMON SPIED MISS BEAUCHAMP outside with her charges the following day. He prayed, took a deep breath, and mustered all the courage he could to apologize for the prank incident.

He willed his legs to move so he could speak with her before recess concluded. Then, after that was settled, he'd head out to a ranch east of town to help mend a fence.

Solomon watched from afar as one of the students said something to Miss Beauchamp. In response, she tossed her head back and a gentle laugh rippled through the air. She obviously had a fine sense of humor and was highly thought of by her pupils. And he would be remiss if he said he hadn't noticed her beauty.

Unfortunate it was that they hadn't met under different circumstances.

He shoved his hands in his trouser pockets and ambled toward her. Practicing the apology last night at his humble abode had sounded ridiculous in his own ears. Would she believe his words?

"Miss Beauchamp?"

She studied him briefly before responding. "Hello, Reverend Solomon."

"Might I speak with you for a moment?"

Before any further words could be spoken, two students rushed toward him, both speaking at once. Frederick's voice, of course, finally drowned out the voice of the other student. "Me and the others were just saying that that was a really good prank you concocted." As if proud of his extensive vocabulary, Frederick paused, slipped his fingers through his suspenders, and peered at the other boy. "Anyhow, it's too bad the pranks are over because I had a really good idea. Maybe you could consider letting us have one more day."

Solomon did not have to meet Lydie's eye to know she was not amused. "Frederick, I appreciate that you're trying to be clever, but..."

Frederick, who needed to work on not interrupting when others were speaking, added more of his thoughts. "Ain't we supposed to be working on developing our minds? If so, we should have another prank day. No offense, Miss Beauchamp."

Both students began to speak again, their excited voices joining together in a boisterous manner in their attempt to persuade Solomon to allow another prank. Miss Beauchamp began to walk away. If Solomon didn't apologize now, he might never work up the courage to do so.

"Miss Beauchamp, please may I speak with you?"

"Reverend Solomon..."

"It will only take a moment, I promise." To the children, he put on his best kind, but firm voice. "Now, students, the prank is only one day. That ensures that it does not become uncontrollable. Please save your ideas for next year."

Miss Beauchamp's eyes widened. He should have mentioned it a different way. "It's of utmost importance," he began, deepening his voice as his pa had done when he was about to say something serious, "to remember we must always obey authority. The prank was to help everyone be at ease on their first day of school..."

Miss Beauchamp set her chin in a stubborn line and raised an eyebrow.

"Well, maybe not everyone would...uh...feel at ease, but..." he had been doing so well without the stuttering until now. He cleared his throat. "Anyhow, we must now be respectful of Miss Beauchamp's authority. As you know, there will be no more pranks or you won't get to participate next year on the prank day." Feeling rather proud of himself for hatching such a brilliant plan, Solomon stood a little straighter and felt braver for the apology that was about to come. Maybe Miss Beauchamp would forgive him after all.

The children moaned, but had the respect to answer, "yes, sir." Miss Beauchamp said nothing, but the perusal of her gaze said she was still not convinced.

"Now go play for the remainder of recess while I speak with your teacher." He motioned for them to join the other students in a game of ball.

Begrudgingly, they did as they were told. And Solomon prayed for courage all over again. "Miss Beauchamp, I reckon..."

"Miss Beauchamp! Miss Beauchamp! Come quickly! Richard is stuck in the tree!"

Solomon followed Miss Beauchamp to the cottonwood tree where the youngest pupil held tightly to a tree branch.

A half-hour later after rescuing Richard, Solomon headed to Mr. Pinson's house. Once again, he hadn't the chance to apologize. He dwelled on it for the first mile. It was important to him that she thought well of him, even if he didn't know her.

But he would like to get to know her.

Preferably with her not thinking of him as the enemy.

When he reached the sizeable Pinson Ranch east of Willow Falls, he noticed a man he presumed to be Abe Pinson near the corral.

"Mr. Pinson?"

"Yes, may I help you?"

Solomon dismounted and extended his hand. "I'm Solomon Eliason. Mr. Morton mentioned you needed help mending your fence."

Mr. Pinson shook his hand. "That I do. Are you a hard worker?"

Memories of the time on the farm flooded his mind. How often had Grandfather called him a "good-for-nothing sluggard"? Too many times to count. This, despite Solomon's best efforts to complete all the work Grandfather assigned him and then some. How many days had he missed school or town events in an attempt to please his grandpa? All for naught. Was he a hard worker? Or was he as Grandfather said?

Mr. Pinson awaited his answer. "Yes, sir, I am a hard worker." For even if Grandfather was right, Solomon could prove himself to Mr. Pinson in this temporary position. He needed the money.

"It's nice to meet you." Mr. Pinson removed his hat, revealing sparse graying hair. His grizzled and leathery face told of time outdoors and his gray handlebar mustache twitched when he spoke. "I just returned from Cheyenne. Lengthy trip from this here northern part of the Territory to the southern part, but with a daughter and her young'uns there, I try to visit when I can." Mr. Pinson stared at Solomon, and he attempted to stand tall in the face of Mr. Pinson's scrutiny. Would he hire him for the job? Would Solomon be able to prove his worth?

"You a God-fearing man, Mr. Eliason?"

"That I am, sir. I'm a reverend, in fact."

"You don't say?"

Solomon prepared himself for the inquiries into how he could possibly be an effective preacher at his age.

"I haven't been to church in Willow Falls in a couple of weeks. Spent some time at my daughter's church in Cheyenne while I was visiting. I do miss Reverend Glenn being here in Willow Falls. He did a right fine job."

"That's what I hear."

Mr. Pinson studied him. "Ain't nothing that says you can't be a good preacher too," he said after some time.

"I hope so, sir." Solomon swallowed the lump in his throat. More than anything, he wanted to be the effective preacher he'd heard Reverend Glenn to be.

"Listen, if you're gonna work for me, why don't you call me 'Abe' and I'll call you 'Reverend Solomon'."

Abe's relaxed nature settled Solomon's unease. "Abe it is."

Lydie tugged her shawl around her shoulders. Already by the time school was released, there was a nip in the air. She'd never minded fall or winter before, but the thought of Christmas without the aunts bothered her.

Christmas in their tiny home in Minnesota, a dwarf pine tree decorated with the handful of ornaments collected over the years in addition to strings of popcorn and cranberries, reminded her of the memorable times she would miss. Would the Castleberrys mind if she spent Christmas with them? While they were cordial and gracious, they weren't family.

Lydie made her way down the boardwalk and toward the Castleberry home. Tonight she would work on the handkerchiefs for the aunts. While she still had ample time before Christmas, she would have to mail them straightaway. There was no telling how long it would take a parcel to reach Prune Creek.

Her mind switched to Reverend Solomon. She had noticed something about him today: that he had kind hazel eyes. Not just "regular" hazel eyes, but nice ones with a rim of gray blue around the edges. Not that she was staring, but he was standing so close.

Goodness, but what was she doing thinking about the reverend's eyes?

His involvement in the pranks did not endear him to her. A man of his age, likely twenty-one or twenty-two, ought to know better. And his statement, *"the prank was to help everyone be at ease on their first day of school"* vexed her greatly. She'd not been at ease that day even before facing sleeping children who all of a sudden became rambunctious hooligans.

The children did seem to like him, even if that was because he instigated mischief.

And he was instrumental in retrieving Richard from the tree, which he'd done with compassion.

She brushed the conflicting thoughts aside. She clearly had no idea what to think of the man or why he had invaded her thoughts.

CHAPTER NINE

SHE RECEIVED CORRESPONDENCE FROM the aunts and she rushed to read their words. They'd both written letters and she read Aunt Myrtle's first.

Dearest Lydie,

I was sorry to hear about your incident at school. The reverend does sound rather brash. Have you had a word with the church elders? Things here are going well. Mr. and Mrs. Peabody are adjusting to our caretaking and living in this large house is quite something. As you recall, it's high on the hill overlooking the valley and not far from town. Fern and I are grateful you secured this position for us.

Aunt Fern seems to be recovering from her heartbreak. Things are so busy here caring for the Peabodys that there is scant time to nurse a broken heart. She is also eating regularly again. Perhaps too regularly.

Please do update us on the happenings at school and with the details of the presumptuous Reverend Solomon.

Love,

Aunt Myrtle

Dearest Lydie,

I, too, was sorry to hear about the incident at school. Who in their right mind would encourage that type of behavior in young scholars?

I hope you are recovering and have not slipped into a melancholy. Remember, Aunt Myrtle and I are just a short ride away should you need us to retrieve you and bring you home. We do miss you something terrible, but are proud of you for becoming a teacher in Willow Falls.

Aunt Myrtle is her same self, a mite bit bossy, but she's doing better with being less overbearing. Wishing I was the eldest will not make it so.

Do write, let us know how you fare, and reassure us that all is well in Willow Falls and with that difficult reverend.

Love,

Aunt Fern

Lydie laughed after reading the letters from the aunts. They were so very protective of her. While Lydie was still a bit irritated with the reverend for his role in the embarrassing and unnerving episode, she had softened to him slightly. She would need to reveal that to her aunts in a future letter lest they worry for her welfare.

She folded the letters and placed them in her bureau for safe keeping. Perhaps she would be able to visit them before the snow flew. From all accounts, the Wyoming Territory had horrendous winters.

She brushed aside the reoccurring reminder that this would be her first Christmas without the aunts.

That Sunday Reverend Solomon was not at church. Mrs. Morton mentioned he had ridden to Nelsonville to preach there, which was customary for the Willow Falls preachers once a month during agreeable weather.

Folks crowded into the church and Mr. Morton from the mercantile did the preaching. He was a nice man, but was not an eloquent speaker. As a matter of fact, Lydie found it difficult to follow his sermon.

Why would so many folks come to hear Mr. Morton, who obviously did not know his Bible as thoroughly as Reverend Solomon, and so few come to listen to a real preacher? Not that Lydie would take the side of the reverend for the episode at the school lingered in her mind. But it did create a question to which she'd like to know the answer.

After Mr. Morton's sermon, everyone met outside for a town meeting with Sheriff Townsend.

The day was perfect for meetings and Lydie hoped for a pleasant and long fall season.

"Thank you, everyone, for attending this short meeting." Sheriff Townsend addressed the crowd with confidence. "While, for the most part, Willow Falls is shielded from the likes of outlaws and ne'er-do-wells, I have received news there is an outlaw gang in the area. They have been robbing stagecoaches and stealing from barns."

Several in attendance gasped and worried wives turned to their husbands. A shiver ran down Lydie's spine. She hadn't given much thought that harm could come to her in Willow Falls. When she and the aunts decided to move to Prune Creek, they knew there were risks in moving to the Wild West from the civilized state of Minnesota. But the aunts, who rarely worried about such things, had prayed for God's protection and not wasted a night's sleep over what might never happen.

Lydie, on the other hand, worried about the outlaws in Prune Creek and during the stagecoach ride to Willow Falls. Frankly, she worried about a lot of things. But this town had seemed so safe and civilized.

"I don't want any of you to worry," said Sheriff Townsend, as if he had read her mind. He then proceeded to give some helpful tips on safety and what to do if anyone saw the men on the wanted poster he passed around.

Lydie would attempt not to worry, but the thought of an outlaw gang in the Willow Falls vicinity weighed heavily on her mind. She fretted about what would happen if they converged on Willow Falls. Would they steal from barns or instigate shootouts in the street by the saloon? Would there be enough able-bodied men to join Sheriff Townsend in apprehending them?

"Fretting does nothing but wear a person down. Waste of time if you ask me." Aunt Myrtle's words sounded in her ears. *"When you worry some, ask God for peace."*

"That's true," added Aunt Fern. *"You might be worrying when you start to pray, but there's no way you can pray and keep worrying at the same time."*

Chapter Ten

SOLOMON STOOD BEHIND THE podium at church on Sunday. He'd been up all night attempting to piece together a lecture that would impress the congregants. He waited for the townsfolk to pile into the church and take their seats in the pews.

He thought of his recent time preaching in Nelsonville. It was a tiny town with only a handful of folks and only three who attended services. It was announced that the town was getting a new reverend, one from Helena in the Montana Territory. It was likely Solomon would only be preaching there one more time before the snow flew and the new preacher arrived.

Once again, he pondered if this was where God wanted him to be.

When it was time to begin services, Solomon attempted to hide his disappointment that only a sparse group of people again sat in the pews. Mr. and Mrs. Morton and Frederick; Sheriff Townsend, his wife, and their young child; Doc and his wife; Abe Pinson; and ironically, Miss Beauchamp—all the same people who attended the first time he'd preached two weeks ago.

His voice faltered in his own ears as he announced the first hymn.

Afterwards, Solomon stood at the door and thanked each person for coming. Miss Beauchamp merely nodded on her way out the door and he reminded himself he still needed to set things to right with her. Between his work at Abe's, working on his sermon, and cleaning the church and parsonage, the remainder of the week had been a flurry of busyness.

Mr. and Mrs. Morton left next, followed by the Townsends. Sheriff Townsend stayed behind while Mrs. Townsend and their young'un waited outside.

"Thank you for the sermon, Reverend," the sheriff said.

Solomon attempted to hide his discouragement. "You're welcome."

As if to read his mind, Sheriff Townsend said, "Don't be disheartened. It'll take some time for folks to warm to the idea of having a new preacher."

"I just hope I'm suitable for the position."

Sheriff Walker Townsend, whom Solomon liked immediately, looked to be a few years older than him. He extended his hand. "You're suitable for whatever it is God calls you to."

"Thanks for the preachin'," Abe said.

"You're welcome. Thank you for coming."

But while each of the four men and the wives of three of them gave accolades, Solomon's dejected thoughts remained unappeased.

Solomon took a seat in a pew after everyone left. While he wouldn't likely starve to death given that he was invited to meals most nights during the week and had leftovers each time, there wasn't enough money in the offering plate to sustain a token salary nor to support missions. Yes, he could easily secure more odd jobs and he liked working hard in the outdoors, but more than anything, he wanted to shepherd a flock and minister to those in need of the Gospel.

With so few parishioners, there wasn't much by way of funds, even if they did give generously. His dreams of purchasing hymnals for the church and funding a ministry in the mining camp in South Pass City would have to wait.

Lord, I thought it was Your will that I come to Willow Falls. Was I wrong in my assumption? Did I misunderstand? He sighed and placed his head in his hands. Maybe Grandfather was right. He'd likely never amount to much. *"What makes you think you have the smarts to be a preacher? You can't even remember to close the barn door. And remember that time you..."*

All of his transgressions he'd ever done while living with Grandfather were laid out that day, as if on a platter. Even if Solomon wanted to forget his mistakes, there was one man who would never allow him to do so.

Had there ever been anything he'd done right in the eyes of his grandfather?

If only his parents had lived. *Why did You take them so soon, Lord? Couldn't You see I needed them? You blessed me with the best parents a boy could have and then took them.* The anguish of losing Ma and Pa had lessened over the years, but it would never fully subside.

Solomon rubbed his temples. If he wasn't able to bring the town together to church, he would need to leave so they could find someone who could. Fall and then winter would be here soon. At that time, travel would be difficult. If Solomon wished to move on, he needed to do so sooner rather than later.

Lord, show me where You can best use me. Guide me, go before me, and lead me. It was his heartfelt prayer he prayed every day, sometimes more than once. *Let me walk worthy of the vocation to which I've been called.*

He knew God heard every prayer and he knew God answered them in His own time.

But the waiting was hard.

"Reverend?"

He lifted his head to see Miss Beauchamp standing beside him. Had she seen him in his dismayed state? Heat rushed up his collar.

And he still needed to apologize about the pranks. Whether Solomon stayed or left Willow Falls behind, that apology must happen.

"Yes, I..."

"Have you seen my brooch? I must have lost it somewhere between here and the Castleberry home where I am staying."

"Your brooch?" Solomon stood. He didn't know much about women's jewelry, but if her brooch was to be found, he would aim to find it. It was the least he could do after the prank ordeal. "Where did you last see it?"

She shared with him the details and together they looked under the pews, then separated and looked around outside and on the way to the Castleberry home and back in search of the lost item. Finally, sometime later as he was about to concede to the brooch being lost forever, Solomon saw something glittering in the September sun.

A brooch.

Solomon retrieved the jewelry and handed it to her. "Would this be it?"

Miss Beauchamp held it to her heart. "Thank you so much, Reverend. This was my Ma's, and I couldn't bear the thought of losing it."

"Glad I could be of help." At least he'd done something right today. He noticed a tear glistening on her cheek. Had she lost her ma too? Suddenly he realized he'd like to know more about her.

But he needed to apologize first. Could he redeem himself?

"Miss…"

"Reverend…"

They both spoke at the same time, and he, recalling his Ma's wise words of being a gentleman deferred to her to speak first.

"I just wanted to say I enjoyed your sermon today."

"You did?"

"Yes."

Her words did something to him he couldn't quite explain. He closed his slack jaw and pondered if he might have heard incorrectly. "Did you say you enjoyed the sermon today?"

"I did."

"My sermon?"

A tiny smile lit her lovely face. "Yes. I believe it was you who was preaching."

"Yes, yes it was. Indeed, it was." Why was he stumbling all over himself like an oaf? Perhaps Miss Beauchamp only offered a compliment because he'd found her brooch.

Still, the compliment shook him. If only he could articulate to her how much her words meant. How they encouraged him. Gave him a miniscule amount of hope that perhaps he was where he needed to be.

"I best be off. Thank you for assisting me with my brooch."

Before he could ask for her forgiveness regarding the prank tradition, Miss Beauchamp rushed toward the Castleberry house.

Dearest Aunt Myrtle and Aunt Fern,

How are you? I am doing well. The students have settled down now that there are no more pranks. Frederick, a young boy of ten, is quite the garrulous child. Alice, another of my students, is very bright, and Richard is my youngest pupil and has two siblings in the school. They recently moved to Willow Falls from Kentucky.

I am shocked to see myself pen these words, but I believe that perhaps Reverend Solomon is not so bad after all. I lost my brooch earlier today and was quite inconsolable at the thought of misplacing one of my two most precious possessions. Imagine my gratitude when the reverend found it after the third time of walking from the church to the Castleberry home. It's a wonder it wasn't stepped on with all of the townsfolk leaving services.

As such, Reverend Solomon has partially redeemed himself in my eyes. However, he still does have yet to apologize for the prank incident. What is peculiar is that not many people attend church in this town. I noticed that as well in Prune Creek. It seems only families attended there as is the case here with the exception of a man named Mr. Pinson. However, when Mr. Morton, one of the elders, preached, many more attended.

I do hope to ask Mrs. Castleberry if she and Mr. Castleberry might attend. Perhaps they are not religious folks; however, they, too, attended when Mr. Morton preached.

Please do write and tell me how you are doing.

With Love,

Lydie

After supper, Mrs. Castleberry took her place near the fireplace with a book. A sizeable parcel full of books had arrived from her former home a few days ago by stage and she'd added it to the bookcase in the parlor. Lydie did her best not to be envious of the plethora of books she'd not yet had the opportunity to read.

She took a seat across from Mrs. Castleberry to work on the handkerchiefs for the aunts.

"Mrs. Castleberry, might I ask a question?"

"You may." The woman glanced up from her book.

Lydie chewed on her lip while simultaneously working up courage. "If you don't mind me asking, is there a reason why you and Mr. Castleberry don't attend church?"

"We attended not long ago."

Lydie couldn't tell if Mrs. Castleberry was irritated with her inquiry. While the woman did put on airs, she was kind and had been gracious to allow Lydie to stay with them. She'd also provided a wide variety of delicious meals and a nice and comfortable room. Perhaps Lydie shouldn't have been so forward. Just as she was about to mention her apologies for asking, Mrs. Castleberry continued.

"It's not that we don't like Reverend Solomon. He seems like an affable young man, but we were accustomed to Reverend Glenn. He had so much maturity and experience. The new reverend..." Mrs. Castleberry's voice trailed. She shook her head and returned to her reading.

Solomon was riding home from helping Mr. Pinson chop wood when an idea struck him. Why not arrange a potluck after church? Didn't everyone come to a celebration when there was food? He was sure Mrs. Townsend, Mrs. Morton, and Mrs. Garrett would bake a dessert. He would arrange it soon since autumn was upon them. Already the crisper weather brought about thoughts of pumpkin pie and apple cider.

A memory of the farm came to mind. Acres upon acres of farmland and pumpkins every year. Grandfather hired a house-keeper who would also bake a delicious pumpkin pie. That was one of only two fond memories Solomon had of his time residing with Grandfather. The other was the time he swam in the creek with some classmates from school. That memory was short-lived when Grandfather let his opinion be known about lazy young men who would rather waste their days swimming than doing chores.

Solomon pushed the thoughts of Grandfather out of his mind. The sun descending behind the mountains, the calm breeze, and the peaceful ride were what he would focus on. He would turn his thoughts to prayer and thank the Lord for all he'd been given.

He was healthy, able-bodied, and had made a few friends in Willow Falls, namely the Townsends, Mr. Pinson, the Mortons, and the Garretts, He had food to eat, water to drink, and shelter.

The outlaw gang, rumored to be in the area, had not been seen. Solomon took extra care during his trip to Nelsonville and kept watch for anything suspicious whenever he was riding to his odd jobs, most of which were outside of town. He was grateful there had been no altercations.

Indeed, Solomon had much to be thankful for.

When he rode into town a few minutes later, he passed by the Castleberry home on his way to the parsonage. Was Miss Beauchamp still angry with him? It bothered him he'd upset her. If only he had given thought before he spoke. And if only he had remembered to meet with the pupils beforehand.

He sighed. At least she had given him a compliment about enjoying his sermon. At first, he thought he'd misheard her.

Even if only those who encouraged him on Sunday benefited or appreciated his sermons, that would have to be enough.

Chapter Eleven

"MISS BEAUCHAMP! MISS BEAUCHAMP!" A breathless Frederick Morton stood in the doorway of the schoolhouse on a sunny late-September day.

Lydie stopped in mid-word from writing on the chalkboard. "Yes, Frederick, what is it?" Had there been an accident? No, Frederick didn't seem distressed. Had a winner been declared for the baseball game?

Frederick dodged toward her and placed his hands on his knees, likely attempting to catch his breath.

"Frederick, is everything all right?"

The boy straightened. "Yes, everything is fine."

"Then what is it?"

"It's the stagecoach. Came into town a few minutes ago."

Lydie couldn't imagine how this might be an emergency. "It sounds as though it's right on time."

"Yes, ma'am, it is."

If there was a line of reasoning to Frederick's excitement, Lydie had surely missed it. "It's about time for recess to conclude."

"But first I gotta tell you something real important."

"Yes?"

"You won't get mad none, will you?" Frederick's brow wrinkled.

Lydie couldn't very well agree not to be angry when she had no idea what he was talking about. Trouble seemed to find Frederick wherever he went because of his curious nature. Thankfully, it was minor shenanigans most of the time. "What happened, Frederick?"

"It's like this. Once upon a time a young boy named Frederick Morton..."

She placed her hands on her hips and prepared to be patient. Frederick was a storyteller and there was no telling how long this tale might be. "Go on..."

"Yes, well as I was sayin', there was a young boy named Frederick Morton. He really liked stagecoaches. As a matter of fact, he wanted to be a stagecoach driver. To fight off the outlaws that made attempts to steal the gold he was haulin'." Frederick did a quick half-turn and made a gun shape with his thumb and pointer finger. "Stay right where you are, mister. There'll be no robbin' the stagecoach on my watch."

He spun back around, his gangly legs too long for his short torso. "So anyway, I was thinkin' as I always do, about stagecoaches. Someone hit the ball real far. Almost to the post office. Of course, I offered to go get it, seeing as how the stage arrives about this time." Frederick pretended to run toward the stagecoach. "Lo and behold, there it was. A thing of beauty. Red with them yellow wheels. Strong horses pullin' it as it drove real fast into town. Dust all kicked up behind it."

"The stagecoach?"

"Yes. And it stopped at the stage stop. I ran past the post office, past the mercantile, and past the saloons. And..." he stared down at his large feet that he hadn't yet grown into. "I ran right past where the ball was hit. But I couldn't help it, Miss Beauchamp. It was all so exciting. Are you sore with me?"

Lydie took a deep breath and was about to detail the importance of staying in the school area when Frederick continued, undeterred. "So then I ran to the stage stop to see who was on it. I keep thinkin' maybe President Ulysses S. Grant will come to Willow Falls someday for a visit. So I done peered toward the stagecoach and three women and one man stepped off. Didn't look like no President Grant, but I hid my disappointment." Frederick stopped briefly enough to take a breath. "But them women, one was the man's wife. The other two, well, I heard them tell the man at the stage stop that they was here to see none other than Miss Beauchamp."

Lydie inhaled, daring to hope. "They did?"

"Yes, ma'am, they did. So, being the helpful fellow I am, I stepped forward and offered up some knowledge. I told 'em I knew where to find Miss Beauchamp. They were pleased as punch when I said that. They asked if you were at the school, and I said, 'yes, she is.' And they said, 'all right, we'll see her after school,' and then they went to the mercantile, probably to stay in that spare room Ma and Pa have that they rent out to visitors until we get a hotel. You ain't mad none are you, Miss Beauchamp?"

Lydie held a hand to her bosom. Aunt Myrtle and Aunt Fern had come for an unexpected visit? "No, Frederick, I am not mad, but please next time stay in the yard." She could barely contain her excitement. "Do tell the children it's time to come back inside for studies." Could she wait two more hours before seeing the aunts?

Patience was a virtue, to be sure, and it would be a struggle to wait.

But wait she would.

As soon as the children left for home, Lydie organized the slates, books, and pencils and ran out the door toward the mercantile.

She lifted her skirts and practically flew down the boardwalk. "Excuse me, excuse me, please," she said to several passersby. How long were the aunts staying? Perhaps she could rent a buggy from the livery and take them around the area to see the fall foliage. Would they be able to stay for the church potluck? She still needed to make the apple pie she promised Mrs. Townsend she'd bring. Were Aunt Myrtle and Aunt Fern at the mercantile? At the stage stop?

But they were at neither. Far ahead, she spied two women sashaying along the boardwalk. Lydie waved, but the two were deep in conversation. She increased her speed, her skirt whipping around her ankles. "Aunt Myrtle! Aunt Fern!"

"Lydie!" The aunts rushed toward her, arms open.

Her throat tightened and she fought the emotion so close to the surface. When she reached them, they enveloped her in a hug. "There, there." Aunt Fern patted her head and Aunt Myrtle squeezed her hand.

Lydie took a step back. "What a pleasant surprise." The tears burned her eyes.

"Yes, well, it's been far too long since we've seen our girl," declared Aunt Myrtle.

"Indeed," agreed Aunt Fern.

"But the distance..." not to mention the cost. The aunts didn't have the kind of funds that allowed such frivolous travel.

Aunt Fern dismissed Lydie's concerns with a wave of her hand. "Pshaw. It's only a short distance over the mountain."

"Will you be staying at the mercantile in their extra room?"

"We will," said Aunt Myrtle. "And we will be here until Monday when we return to Prune Creek."

Lydie wanted to ask if they would be interested in moving to Willow Falls, but she knew they were content in their new home, especially now in their roles as caregivers.

"We can't leave the Peabodys alone for long. Their daughter and son-in-law are there for a visit for the next few days. That allowed us to come visit you." Aunt Fern draped an arm around Lydie's shoulders. "We've been so troubled over the situation with that insolent reverend. Tell us, how are you faring?"

"I'm fine, Aunt Fern."

Aunt Myrtle eyed her with skepticism, head tilted slightly. "We certainly hope that to be the case."

The boardwalk boasted plentiful passersby on their way hither and yon. Lydie stepped in front of the aunts as they could not all walk side-by-side on the narrow footpath.

They were nearing the mercantile, Lydie's focus behind her so as to listen to the aunts. As such, she wasn't watching where she was going. Suddenly and without warning, she ran directly into something. Or someone.

Lydie turned and her eyes connected with his and her stomach did a peculiar lurch. "Oh, Reverend, I'm so sorry."

"Goodness, but is this the brash and insolent Reverend Solomon who plays pranks on teachers and encourages young'uns to do the same?" Aunt Myrtle stepped ahead of Lydie.

"Ma'am..." began Reverend Solomon.

"Such a disagreeable fellow," added Aunt Fern.

Aunt Myrtle's brow furrowed and she tsked. "What kind of person, and a reverend at that, would conceive such outlandish shenanigans?"

"Make sure you make your thoughts clear on the matter, Myrtle," said Aunt Fern.

"Oh, I aim to. Young man, why on earth would you do such a thing? Our poor Lydie was panic-stricken."

Lydie held her breath. If there was one thing a person ought to know, it was that you never wanted to land on the wrong side of Aunt Myrtle and Aunt Fern.

"Ma'ams, please, I can explain." Reverend Solomon fiddled with the button on his sleeve. "I've been meaning to explain the whole thing to Miss Beauchamp."

Lydie would very much like to hear the reverend's excuse for the disquietude he caused her. She leaned forward a bit.

But the aunts would have none of it. "You should be ashamed," admonished Aunt Myrtle.

"I don't always agree with my sister, but this time I wholeheartedly do," added Aunt Fern. "Now, let's be on our way. We have much catching-up to do with Lydie. Good day, Reverend."

Lydie almost felt sorry for the man. Perhaps there was an explanation. She and the aunts continued their stroll toward the room at Morton's Mercantile for an early supper.

"I'm grateful you arrived safely. Sheriff Townsend was telling us about an outlaw gang wanted for robbing stagecoaches and stealing from people's barns." Lydie shivered.

Aunt Fern finished chewing her food and dabbed at her mouth. "The driver mentioned something similar about a gang near Willow Falls. We worried for a bit, then handed it over to the Lord. Fortunately, the journey here was without incident. The driver told us before we left that one of his fellow drivers over near the Poplar Springs area has been robbed each time on his route." Aunt Fern shook her head. "Poor passengers. The one time the robbers managed to get away with not only money and mail, but also the personal belongings from some of the travelers, including an expensive hat from a woman on the stage. Can you imagine losing your new hat in a stagecoach robbery?"

Aunt Myrtle glowered. "Apparently, she'd just purchased it. Tsk tsk. Do robbers have nothing better to do than to take things that belong to others?"

"Please do be careful on the return trip," said Lydie. While the aunts brushed worry aside, Lydie found it more difficult to do so.

"Oh, we shall. Just have some of Aunt Myrtle's homemade goodies, offer them out to the robbers, and they'll perish straightaway." Aunt Fern clasped her hands. "Problem eliminated."

Aunt Myrtle tossed a glare her sister's way. "Likely not. You're the only one who doesn't appreciate my cooking, Fern."

Lydie and Aunt Fern passed a knowing glance. Unfortunately for Aunt Myrtle, Aunt Fern was not the only one who disliked her cooking.

CHAPTER TWELVE

"I'M POSITIVELY GIDDY ABOUT making a pie for the potluck," declared Aunt Myrtle early the next morning as they strolled down the boardwalk after breakfast. The tour of the town took ten minutes.

Lydie and Aunt Fern exchanged a glance and Aunt Fern expressed her thoughts aloud. "I can say with complete honesty that no one is going to be positively giddy about eating the pie."

"Pshaw. That's balderdash if you ask me. Just because I forgot to add sugar one time does not mean I'm incapable of baking an award-winning pie. Besides, I have just the idea for the filling since apparently there are no blueberries to be had in the wilds of the Wyoming Territory."

That was one thing Lydie appreciated about Aunt Myrtle. Her tenacious personality. She never gave up easily. "What is your idea, Aunt Myrtle?"

"Glad you asked. You see, I was talking to the man at the stage stop yesterday and he mentioned there were huckleberries growing here. The season for picking them is over, but fortunately for me, Mrs. Morton has a bucket she has saved for a special occasion. When I mentioned I was known for my baking skills, she said I may have some for a pie if I'd like to make one for the potluck. She also offered me use of her stove since the room we are boarding in doesn't have one." Aunt Myrtle held her chin high and pressed a hand to smooth her braided hair that wound around her head at least twice. "I recall her exact words. She said, 'would you and your sister like to bake something for the potluck?' To which, I replied with a resounding 'yes!' Not to sound prideful, mind you, but I assure you, Lydie, that once the fine folks of Willow Falls discover your aunt's culinary skills, they will accept you all the more."

Aunt Fern reared her head back and pressed her lips together. "We're to be helping Lydie be an accepted member of the community, not banished permanently."

"Oh, hush, Fern."

But Fern instead laughed, her contralto voice carrying on the breeze. "Well, I've never tasted huckleberries. I dare say I must try some *before* Myrtle bakes her *scrumptious* pie."

Lydie reveled in the time spent with the aunts. Even if they brabbled.

With the addition of Miss Beauchamp's ornery aunts, the total of those attending church was twelve. Solomon preached from the book of Isaiah, his voice sounding strained in his own ears. When the service concluded, he announced about the potluck.

As he stood at the door shaking hands with the few parishioners, Solomon caught a glimpse of several townsfolk milling around outside, apparently eager for the potluck. He once again hoped that someday he would earn the approval of the people he'd come to serve.

"Hello, Reverend. Excellent sermon as usual." Abe shook his hand.

"Thank you, sir." He had come to appreciate Abe's kindness and his wisdom.

"Look at all that food." Abe patted his belly and strolled toward the festivities with a bowlegged gait.

Mr. Morton, Sheriff Townsend, and Doc helped set up makeshift tables and several women had lined them with all types of delicacies including chicken, beans, and pies. Solomon's stomach growled.

Sheriff Townsend patted Solomon on the back. "It looks like your plan for a potluck is a success. Care to join me for something to eat?" He lowered his voice. "Candace brought the mock turtle soup, and I can tell you that it'll be the best thing here."

Solomon had never tasted mock turtle soup, but knew from his experience eating at the Townsend home that Candace Townsend was a talented cook.

He led a prayer to bless the meal and everyone partook in the numerous food items lining the tables. Solomon had just finished his last bite of mock turtle soup when Miss Beauchamp and her aunts wandered toward him. He sure wished Miss Beauchamp would forgive him for his error. Perhaps he would have the opportunity today to garner the courage to speak with her about it and seek her forgiveness.

Certainly, there had not been an opportunity in which to speak to her, but also, if he were honest, Solomon would have to admit he was procrastinating.

What if she didn't forgive him?

What if she held his offense against him?

He saw her from his peripheral. Was it his imagination or did she give him the stink eye?

"Reverend Solomon," said the taller of the aunts, "you must try the huckleberry pie."

"Huckleberry pie?" He'd never tasted that particular berry before, but he had eyed the apple pie sitting near the edge with only one slice left.

The aunt nodded. "Yes. I hear huckleberries grow in the Wyoming Territory, and I was fortunate enough that Mrs. Morton had some to spare before she begins canning them."

"I've not tasted huckleberries before, ma'am. I'm from Minnesota and northern Iowa. I've had my share of blueberries and blackberries, however."

The other aunt, the quieter one, gasped. "You are from Minnesota?"

"Yes, ma'am. Moved there with my grandfather as a young'un."

"You don't say." Her already large eyes grew larger and she stared at him as if to discern whether or not he spoke the truth. "I am astounded. You see, we are from Minnesota as well."

They spoke for a few minutes about the state when the other aunt cleared her throat. "Do excuse me for a minute, Fern. May someone else get a word in?" She paused before continuing. "Would you like to try a piece of huckleberry pie, Reverend?"

Solomon could likely eat several huckleberry pies. He recalled Ma's words all those years ago about how he surely was growing because of how much he ate. "I'd be much obliged, Miss...Aunt..."

"Aunt Myrtle." She rushed over to the table to an untouched purplish pie. She cut him a generous slice and plopped it on his plate. "Shall I cut a second slice?"

The woman was presumptuous, but Solomon figured he'd likely want another slice. He eyed the popular apple pie again. If no one else wanted that last slice, he'd eagerly take it too.

Solomon's mouth watered. He sawed at the crust, noting it was a little tough to cut. Perhaps that's how it was with huckleberry pies. He shrugged and continued until he'd attained a decent-sized bite. The crust, darker than any crust he'd ever seen, appeared almost black. Maybe that was because of the plentiful huckleberries.

"Did you put sugar in it?" the other aunt asked Aunt Myrtle.

"Hush, Fern. You know I did. That was only one time that I didn't put sugar in."

"Dear Lord, bless this meal this reverend is about to eat and keep him and all safe who consume this pie." After the aunt prayed, she added, "Not that many will consume it. Of that, I am sure."

He almost chuckled aloud. Miss Beauchamp's aunts were amusing, but should he be concerned that the shorter aunt thought not many would consume the pie? Should he ask what she meant by that before eating it?

"By the way, I'm Aunt Fern. The one with the baking skills." The shorter aunt nodded toward him. "And Myrtle's younger and more pleasant sister."

He paused before taking a bite. "Nice to meet you."

"Nice to have known you too."

Aunt Myrtle elbowed her. "Quit it, Fern. You're being loathsome."

Aunt Fern only laughed. "Am I being loathsome, Lydie?"

"Don't you dare take her side like you did that time during the county fair," warned Aunt Myrtle.

Solomon's fork remained suspended in the air. Dare he take a bite?

"You're not being loathsome, Aunt Fern," said Lydie. She giggled, a soft pleasing giggle. So distracted he was that he almost dropped the huckleberry pie bite off his fork.

Aunt Myrtle's eyebrows drew downward in a frown. "Best you eat that bite, young man, before it falls on the ground and wastes all my hard work."

"Yes, ma'am." Solomon expected it to melt in his mouth, given the aroma of fresh berries that waffled toward his nose.

However, it was neither delicious nor savory. It did not melt in his mouth and he pondered briefly if it was fit for human consumption. The aroma of the pie had been deceitful and he nearly gagged.

"Isn't it delicious?" Aunt Myrtle asked.

When Solomon saw her expression, he knew for certain she was not being facetious. She genuinely appeared to want him to enjoy the huckleberry pie. How could he tell her his thoughts without hurting her feelings? He couldn't lie.

Revulsion started in his throat and worked its way to his mouth. He gulped, swallowed a portion, gulped again, felt his eyes water, then swallowed the bite of pie.

"Well?" Aunt Myrtle asked expectantly.

"I...I...well, it's..." Miss Beauchamp tilted her head and he thought he saw the beginning of a smile. Not a laugh as though he was being mocked, but a genuine smile. He gulped again. Perhaps someone had thought to bring a pitcher of lemonade. "It's...well...it's like nothing I've tasted before."

Aunt Myrtle released a breath. "I knew you'd like it. It's my first time making it, but I could tell just from its appearance that it would be delectable."

Delectable was not a word he would use to describe this pie. Did he imagine it or was there gratitude in Lydie's countenance?

"Well, I'm thankful you liked it, Reverend," added Aunt Myrtle. "I wasn't sure it was going to turn out right when I realized I'd put in a bigger pinch of salt than the recipe called for."

No wonder it had tasted salty and bitter. Solomon glanced at his plate at the large uneaten piece of pie that remained. Surely, he would not have to finish it. Not that he wished to waste, but he hadn't tasted anything so awful in his life. And upon closer examination, he noticed the burnt crust. Solomon's eyes darted toward the apple pie. "Might I have that last piece of pie if it's not spoken for?" he asked.

Thankfully, the rest of the attendees were mingling and hadn't been privy to the huckleberry pie debacle.

"Oh, yes, Lydie made that pie," said Aunt Fern. She took Solomon's plate from him, shoved aside the repulsive huckleberry pie, and plopped the slim piece of apple pie beside it.

Without acting like he was about to die and in need of something to take away the taste of the huckleberry pie, Solomon, as calmly as possible, cut a piece of the apple pie. He chewed it slowly, relishing the delicious taste, so opposite from the first pie. "This is very good," he said after he swallowed the bite.

"Of course it is," quipped Aunt Fern. "Lydie gets her baking skills from me."

CHAPTER THIRTEEN

IT WAS THE THIRD person in the jail Solomon had visited upon Sheriff Townsend's request since he arrived in Willow Falls. The other two men hadn't cared about what Solomon had to say, and he figured this man would be no different.

Still, he knew this was part of his calling. He was to plant the seeds. How they were cultivated was up to the Lord.

He was surprised, however, that Sheriff Townsend continued to ask him to speak with the prisoners given his record.

"Campbell is in for disorderly conduct," Sheriff Townsend was telling him as they entered the jail. Solomon offered another prayer, his fourth on the matter, before settling into the uncomfortable chair near the lone cell. The sheriff took his place behind his desk.

"Hello, Mr. Campbell, I'm Reverend Solomon."

The prisoner, who looked to be in his thirties, stood and gripped the bars. He gawped at Solomon, his eyes tightened at the corners. "So you're the preacher. Don't look older than a youngster."

Solomon tamped down the frustration that lit every time someone said something similar. Maybe he ought to grow a beard. Wear spectacles. Gain a few pounds around the middle.

Anything to make him appear more seasoned. "I hear you're in for disorderly conduct."

"That's what the sheriff said." Campbell's greasy hair, in need of a good washing, hung in thin uneven strands near the base of his neck, as if the barber was asleep when he cut it. He looked down his long, crooked nose at Solomon. "Suppose you're here to tell me to live a better life. Get some religion and all that. 'Course, a man like you don't know the first thing about hardships. Probably had a perfect life with a perfect ma and pa and all that."

Solomon shifted in his chair, wishing the tall lanky man would take a seat on the cot rather than loom over him. "A godly ma and pa, yes. But they died when I was just a young'un, and I was raised by my grandfather." An image of Grandfather's scowling face entered his mind. "*Ain't never gonna amount to nothin', Solomon, if you don't learn to do something right.*"

"Lucky you. Never knew my grandfather."

Solomon pushed aside the thoughts that his life would have been better if he hadn't known his, but such thoughts weren't charitable and definitely not the thoughts of a man of the cloth. "My grandfather is a hard man. I have never done anything right in his eyes."

"I got me a pa like that." The man's demeanor shifted from arrogant to lamentable and he finally took a seat on the cot. He extended his long skinny legs in front of him and picked at a scab on his hand. "I don't think he ever liked me. Ma weren't much better. She has my sister and that's all that matters."

"Grandfather owns a farm in Minnesota. He had me working it since I went to live with him, but he was persnickety in his ways."

"Persnickety. Hmm. Sounds like Pa. He's a wagonmaker, a skilled one at that. Not me. When I didn't want to follow in his footsteps and be a wagonmaker too, he called me every unkind name you can think of. I had me enough of that and went my own way.

Solomon nodded and thought a minute before he spoke. Were his words even helping? The last thing he wanted was to share about his own life. A verse from Second Corinthians popped into his mind: "...*that we may be able to comfort them which are in any trouble, by the comfort wherewith we ourselves are comforted of God.*"

God *had* comforted Solomon in the daily trials of attempting to please a man who neither loved him nor cared about him. The Lord *had* given Solomon the strength to endure Grandfather's harsh words and belittling, mean-spirited actions.

Could Solomon now assist someone else who had a similar story? Would his words matter to the man who sat staring at him from the other side of the bars? He shifted in his chair. "Grandfather wanted me to be a farmer, which I enjoyed several aspects of, but I knew there was a different calling on my life." He ran his hand over his Bible. Now after having moved to Willow Falls, he wasn't so sure God was truly calling him to the pulpit. Maybe he ought to return to Minnesota and work on the farm again. Grandfather would tell him he had failed, that he was a ne'er-do-well, that he'd been right when he said Solomon would be an inferior preacher. He'd make Solomon beg and grovel for Grandfather to take him back.

How could all of that be comforting to the inmate before him?

Solomon offered a prayer for guidance and gazed about the room. Sheriff Townsend had leaned back in his chair, feet on the desk, and hands clasped behind his head. Campbell fidgeted again, but sat a little straighter on the cot.

"Ain't you got more to say?" Campbell asked.

This wasn't about him. It wasn't about Grandfather. It wasn't about the burden he carried like a heavy weight on his back that never relented. It was about being a different kind of farmer. A farmer who planted a seed and gave the growing of it to God. But how could he do so without offering a lecture? He'd tried that twice now with the two former prisoners. It hadn't worked.

"I'm glad God isn't like my grandfather," Solomon finally said.

"Who says He ain't?"

"His Word."

The man howled with laughter, his bean-shaped nostrils flaring as he chortled a laugh that echoed in the dusty jail. "You and I both know He's sittin' up there in Heaven being no different than my pa and your grandfather. Just waitin' for us to mess up. Just knowin' we ain't worth nothin'."

Solomon sat for a moment and waited to speak. His first inclination was to prove Campbell wrong. His second, wiser inclination was to pause before using this opportunity to share the Truth.

"I don't know about your pa, but I've never known if my grandfather loves me," he said, the words biting into his heart as he said them. "I know God does not leave evil unpunished, and He is a God of justice. He has to be since He's holy."

Campbell's lips curled and he cracked his knuckles. "'Course. Don't that sound just like God. Ready to punish."

"I also know other things about God."

"Oh, you do, do you? Like what?" The man crossed his hands across his chest. "Is this where you start preachin'?"

Solomon flipped through the pages of his Bible where he had meticulously underlined certain passages. For the next several minutes, he shared several of those verses, alternating with his own personal experiences, and finally his testimony. "My parents taught me about Jesus' sacrifice on the Cross. I may have repented of my sins and made Jesus my Lord and Savior at a young age, and I have been walking with Him most of my life, but that doesn't mean I'll ever be perfect this side of Heaven. I still make mistakes and still need forgiveness from a Holy God. But He tells me in His Word that He'll never leave me nor forsake me. My grandfather has all but disowned me. He has left and forsaken me. But God never will." He lowered his voice and said more to himself than to Campbell, "How many times have I reminded myself of this?" Solomon tamped down the pain of Grandfather's spitefulness. The ache pressed against his chest and he wished he could have been the grandson Grandfather wanted.

Campbell didn't say a word, but instead scrutinized him. "You truly believe all this? What Jesus did, this forgiveness stuff, and that God will never leave you?"

"I do."

From his peripheral, Solomon saw Sheriff Townsend watching them. There wasn't a sound in the jail besides the ticking of the clock. Several minutes passed and Solomon wondered if he ought to have said less. Or something different. Or let someone more experienced speak with Campbell.

"Do you think God is choosy in who He helps?"

"You don't have to be someone special to come to Him. As a matter of fact, I think He prefers those who are broken and know they need a Savior. 'Come unto me, all ye that labour and are heavy laden, and I will give you rest.'"

Campbell bent forward. "Is that what the Bible says?"

"It does."

"And He'll give me rest?"

Solomon nodded. He prayed, no *begged* for the right words to say. "I can help you find new life in Him."

"But I don't have me a Bible."

Solomon peered down at his beloved and worn Bible. Despite his best intentions, it had become frayed on the edges. Despite his doting care for it, the spine of the book had creases in it. "You can have mine." He handed it to Campbell through the bars.

Campbell blinked and took the Bible from him. "Are you sure?"

"I'm sure. That is, if you don't mind that it has some of the verses underlined in pencil."

"I don't mind at all." Campbell thrummed through the pages. "Helps to have some of them verses underlined. Then I know where to start, seein' as how I'm gonna be here for a few days."

Solomon waited for Campbell to say more, and when he didn't Solomon rose. "It was nice to meet you, Mr. Campbell. I'll stop back by tomorrow."

But Campbell didn't answer. His head was bent as he read the words of the only book that could truly change a life.

CHAPTER FOURTEEN

LYDIE STEPPED INSIDE THE Castleberry home. After closing the door behind her, she unbuttoned her coat and hung it by the door. She inhaled a delectable aroma and wondered what tasty dessert Mrs. Castleberry's hired help made today.

She yearned to spend time in her room before supper with one of the books Mrs. Castleberry loaned her, and after supper, pen a letter to the aunts.

"Lydie, is that you?" Mrs. Castleberry called from the parlor.

Instead of ascending the stairs, Lydie strolled toward the parlor where Mrs. Castleberry was sitting in one of the chairs and Mrs. Symons, a woman from town, in the other.

"Do come in and join us." Mrs. Castleberry gestured to the settee.

Disappointed in the deviation from her original plan, but not wanting to present herself as being rude, Lydie took a seat on the settee and reached for her latest sewing project.

Mrs. Castleberry pointed to a plate of pastries on the table. "Do have a pastry, dear. Have you made Mrs. Symons's acquaintance?"

Before Lydie could answer, Mrs. Symons interjected. "Yes, I've met Lydie. My youngest daughter attends the Willow Falls School."

Lydie took a dainty bite of the pastry. "How was school today?" Mrs. Castleberry asked.

"The students are doing so well with their recitation. We've been working on poetry and the Psalms." Lydie was exceptionally proud of how quickly her pupils memorized the material they were taught.

"Yes, well," began Mrs. Symons, "that is all good and well, but I for one am grateful my youngest is the only one attending school in Willow Falls. My eldest and second child both received quality educations in Chicago before my husband decided he needed to try his hand at ranching in the Wyoming Territory."

Mrs. Castleberry nodded as if she understood. "I always did wonder what brought you to the uncivilized West. I do understand about the quality of education. I'm thankful my daughter has since completed her book learning."

Lydie's confidence fell. What if other parents thought she was doing an inadequate job? She bit her lip and allowed worry to niggle its way inside her mind. What did the school board think of her performance as a teacher? She suddenly had no appetite and placed the half-eaten pastry respectfully on the plate.

"This town is far too unrefined if you ask me," said Mrs. Symons. "If Barry hadn't set his sights on owning the largest ranch in the area, we would still be in Chicago with the theater, fine schools, and quality religious services. I'd also have my lovely mansion, rather than the hovel in which I must now reside."

While the Symons home was not near as elaborate as the Castleberry home, it *was* a resplendent home and far from a hovel.

"Yes, the religious services. Mr. Castleberry and I spoke of this topic the day before last. Reverend Solomon is too young and too unversed."

"Yes, and he's nothing like Reverend Glenn. Now that man had a gift for preaching." Mrs. Symons shook her head. "Maybe he can return when he has some experience. Did the elders even know how young he was when they hired him? He could be our son."

While Lydie didn't cotton to Reverend Solomon's decision to enlist children in ridiculous pranks, she didn't believe he deserved the treatment being doled out to him. He didn't deserve such petty talk, especially when he wasn't here to defend himself.

Aunt Fern's words of wisdom came to mind. *"There's no room in a godly woman's life for talebearing. The Good Book tells us, 'Where no wood is, there the fire goeth out: so where there is no talebearer, the strife ceaseth.'"*

Should Lydie excuse herself and take her leave?

Mrs. Symons adjusted the quilt she was sewing. "I do declare that our family has ceased attending services since Reverend Solomon arrived. We can't have someone preaching to the flock who has no life experience himself. How can we expect him to be able to help others with the situations in which they find themselves when he's never experienced those things himself? How is my daughter supposed to get the spiritual nourishment she needs?"

"Mr. Castleberry and I attended the one service he preached at, but didn't return. Such a shame as we are to fellowship. I fear if something isn't done posthaste, we shall not have a church at all in this town." She sighed. "What do you think, Lydie?"

Lydie fiddled with Ma's brooch.

"Yes, do tell us what you think," said Mrs. Symons. She stared down her long, pointed nose at Lydie. Her pinched mouth and sour expression told more than her words ever could.

Mrs. Castleberry took a sip of her tea. "You've been attending regularly, have you not?"

Lydie moistened her lips. "I have."

"Go on," encouraged Mrs. Castleberry.

"I do believe we should give him an ample chance. He is new, after all." Lydie lamented the squeakiness in her voice. It was doubtful her tone would convince the women.

Mrs. Symons stared at her with haughty disapproval. "Poppy-cock! He's been given a chance. He's not Reverend Glenn and that is that."

Lydie's irritation spiked. If asked, no one would ever say boldness and courage described her. But Aunt Myrtle and Aunt Fern had taught her many things in her growing-up years. And while she should not have allowed herself to voice her thoughts without thinking twice, some things needed to be said. "I don't know who Reverend Glenn is, but I do know that if you have a concern about Reverend Solomon's preaching, the Christian way to go about it is to discuss it with him. Not gossip about him when he isn't present. Besides, how do you expect him to succeed at his calling if you don't give him the opportunity to practice?"

The expressions on the women's faces indicated she quite possibly had spoken out of turn. Mrs. Symons's words confirmed it.

"You, Miss Beauchamp, are quite possibly one of the brashest young ladies I have ever had the misfortune of encountering." She stood, gathered her items, tossed one more hoity-toity glare at Lydie, bid Mrs. Castleberry goodbye, then left.

Lydie's eyes stung and she sat for a moment in silence with Mrs. Castleberry. Would the woman determine she ought not stay there any longer? Would she recommend to the school board that Lydie be relieved of her duties as a teacher? The Castleberrys had much influence in Willow Falls, and their word would be taken seriously. Would Lydie fail at the job she so desperately loved when she'd been there such a short time? Her chest tightened in fear at all she could lose just from allowing her words to get the best of her. Worry gnawed at her and she lifted a prayer heavenward.

Awkward silence filled the room and Mrs. Castleberry folded her hands in her lap and stared at something on the wall.

Should she apologize to Mrs. Castleberry? Would the woman forgive her for speaking her mind? Should she offer to speak with Mrs. Symons and rectify things? She glanced at the pastry. The only sounds in the room were the pounding of her own heartbeat and the crackling of the fire. Mr. Castleberry would be home soon and she wouldn't have the chance to set things to right. She took a deep breath and prayed for guidance. "Mrs. Castleberry, I am so sorry I upset you and Mrs. Symons."

Mrs. Castleberry said nothing and seconds ticked by. Tears misted Lydie's eyes and she blinked. Should she excuse herself and retire to her room?

After an extended amount of time, Mrs. Castleberry finally spoke. "Well, I do declare, Lydie. I never thought you to be one to speak her mind. You are so soft-spoken and timorous."

"I'm so sorry, Mrs. Castleberry, if I've cost you a friend."

"Well, you may have your own opinions, just as Mrs. Symons may have hers." Mrs. Castleberry sighed. "I've been deliberating your words. Perhaps they have some merit."

Lydie excused herself, retrieved the plate with the pastry, and hastened from the room before tears brimming at the surface slid down her face.

Chapter Fifteen

The following day, Solomon visited Campbell again in the jail. He prayed with him to accept Christ as his Savior. It was a humbling event and Solomon wasn't sure at first that he would be able to focus on anything else for the remainder of the day.

But there was something else on his mind as he rode his horse out of town and to Abe's house to assist on his ranch.

When he'd left the jail, Sheriff Townsend had asked to speak with him in private.

"The elders would like to meet with you tomorrow at Morton's."

The words rang through his mind over and over. Sheriff Townsend hadn't elaborated because he'd been interrupted by a skirmish at the saloon.

Leaving Solomon to wonder what the conversation would consist of.

"Seems like you're carrying around a burden today," Abe commented that afternoon as he and Solomon sat at the table for the noonday meal.

Solomon had grown closer to Abe in the past several days as he assisted the older man on his ranch. So much so that Abe had become like a mentor to him. He shared with him about the life-changing news about Campbell. But should he share the concerns that weighed on him?

"Reckon it's not gonna get much better if you hold it all inside." Abe scooped a second helping onto Solomon's plate.

"Sheriff Townsend said the elders want to meet with me tomorrow."

Abe nodded. "Ah, that's what's got you concerned. Did he say why?"

"No, but I think it may have to do with the fact that I haven't had many parishioners at church since I arrived." Solomon pushed around the food on his plate with his fork.

"Doesn't mean it has to be something bad, does it?"

Abe had a point.

"I know that there's been a few of the townsfolk complaining that I don't have the experience or knowledge to shepherd a flock. I know Mr. Symons made a complaint to Doc the other day."

"Mr. Symons is a rabblerouser." Abe scooped up his last bite of beans. "I know you've prayed for the Lord's leading."

"Yes. I'm not sure that this is where He has called me to be. At first, I thought it was, but now..."

Abe pushed his plate aside and steepled his fingers. "Unfortunately, there will always be those who don't like us. I'm sure you're familiar with the verse in Galatians where Paul says if he seeks to please men, he would not be a servant of Christ."

Solomon was familiar with the verse. "Yes, but..." he took a deep breath. "I do want the townsfolk to like me."

"Of course. Who wouldn't want others to like us? But we shouldn't aim to please people. There's only One we need to please. His opinion is the only one that matters."

"You're right, Abe, it's just that with Grandfather thinking I'll fail at this and now with the real possibility I might..." Solomon could see Grandfather's expression if he discovered Solomon wasn't welcome to preach in Willow Falls.

Abe sat up straight in his chair. "I know your grandfather is a hard man. What he's done to you isn't right. But you have a willing heart and God uses willing hearts for His purposes. He doesn't use willing hearts to please the Willow Falls townsfolk or willing hearts to please Grandfather. He uses willing hearts for *His* purposes. To further *His* kingdom. Just like you did today with Campbell. When we submit to His Lordship, humble ourselves, and give our lives to Him with an open hand, His will will be done."

The kindness and benevolence in Abe's eyes, coupled with his wisdom and forthright nature made Solomon respect him all the more. "I know you're right, Abe. It's just that I really want to succeed at leading the flock here in Willow Falls, but what if that's not God's will? More than anything I want it to be His will."

"Of course, you do. You have a passion for leading others and for sharing from God's Word. You have a servant's heart and an eager spirit. God will direct you, but it will be His will. And if it is His will that you remain in Willow Falls as the reverend, no one, not Mr. Symons or anyone else, will be able to thwart God's plans."

Abe was right. But it was a challenge to completely dismiss the doubts that crowded his mind. Doubts that he wasn't good enough.

"Besides," added Abe. "I think you do a fine job. You're young, yes. But I'd rather have someone with an eagerness than a hard-headed and prideful fellow set in his ways."

"But everyone respected Reverend Glenn. How can I compare to him?"

"You can't because you're not him. Reverend Glenn was about a hundred years old if he was a day. Gracious fellow who knew the Bible forward and back. I know it's hard not to compare yourself to him, but doing so won't make matters any better."

Solomon hoped to someday have as much wisdom as Abe. "How come you never became a preacher?"

"Me?" Abe chuckled. "I couldn't speak in front of a crowd. Too nervous when it comes to all those people watching me. Besides, that's not what God called me to do."

Lydie arrived to find Reverend Solomon stacking wood in the schoolhouse. He must have also lit the stove because warmth filled the air. "Thank you, Reverend." Had he spoken to the other school board members? She'd not heard a word from any of them yet regarding her possible faux pas with Mrs. Symons.

He stacked the last remaining logs. "You're welcome."

It was then that she noticed just how threadbare his coat was. She saw glimpses of his plaid shirt beneath the frayed fabric. Was it because he was unable to afford a new one given the inability of the parishioners to support a preacher? Her heart hurt at the thought. No one ought to be cold.

When he finished, he stood and unfolded his height from its lowered position. His arms stood slack at his sides and something about his demeanor was different than she'd seen previous times. He didn't stand as straight as usual, and the twinkle of orneriness she'd seen in his eyes was absent. "I have a meeting at Morton's this morning, so thought I would stop here on my way."

A meeting at Morton's? She held her breath. Would the meeting be about her and her conversation with Mrs. Symons? Should she ask?

"Miss Beauchamp, there's something I need to speak with you about." His apprehensive expression gave her pause. Would he be the one to discuss with her the situation with Mrs. Symons?

But before she could respond, Frederick rushed through the front door. "Reverend Solomon! I was hoping you'd be here." He and Richard bounded toward the reverend. "I have something to tell you." Frederick, as usual, continued in a rush of a million words a minute before catching his breath. Several other students had gathered around, all greeting Reverend Solomon in the midst of Frederick's ardent diatribe.

A grin of amusement lit the reverend's face and his solemn countenance relaxed.

"And then when I opened the box, you can't believe what I saw. It was the best toys. All shipped to my pa's mercantile. And he said I could try them out before we put them on the shelves!"

Richard frowned. "Not fair. Wish my pa owned the mercantile."

Several other students competed against Frederick's voice with their own interjections.

"If my pa owned the mercantile, I'd ask to try all the beautiful dresses," Alice swirled around in a circle.

"Not me. I would eat all of the licorice. Then I'd eat the gumdrops. I once tasted those when we lived in Kansas."

Amusement flickered in Reverend Solomon's eyes and his mouth quirked with humor. "I recall once when I was a boy."

It was all he needed to say and the children, even Frederick, offered their rapt attention. The image of the students peering up at the preacher, awaiting what he might say, tugged at Lydie's heart. The man had a way with children.

"What is it, Reverend Solomon? What is your memory?" Frederick's brown eyes gleamed with anticipation.

"When my pa and I went into town one time, we were to retrieve Ma when she was finished at the quilting bee. We stopped at the mercantile because we needed to find something special for Ma for Christmas. It wasn't an easy task because Ma never told us what she'd like. We always had to guess."

"Sounds like my ma," piped up one of the children.

Reverend Solomon chuckled and continued. "That and Ma always liked to come with us, so there was no sneaking and finding the perfect gift. Pa suggested this would be a good time to stop at the mercantile since Ma was busy quilting and babbling on with the womenfolk."

Richard raised his hand. "My ma likes to babble too."

"Yes, well, my ma attended the quilting bee once a month, and Pa and I figured we were safe to sneak into the mercantile since she and her friends were chatty sorts who talked into the next century."

Lydie laughed at Reverend Solomon's words. Aunt Myrtle and Aunt Fern could easily talk into the next century and then some.

"So we looked around the mercantile for just the perfect gift. Ma wasn't picky, but she *was* particular. We settled on this porcelain doll. Pa had the doll in his arms and was about to carry it to the counter when we noticed a very familiar woman lurking around the corner near the sewing notions."

"Was it your ma?" one of the younger students asked.

"Just wait and let the reverend tell it," Alice admonished.

The warmth of Reverend Solomon's smile echoed in his voice. "Ma noticed us, but I think she pretended not to. She turned away rather abruptly, walked a few steps in the opposite direction and busied herself with some horse tack against the far wall. Well, Pa knew as well as I did that horse tack never interested Ma. Her tastes lie more akin to fabrics and dishes." He paused as if reliving the memory in his mind. "Pa still clutched that doll, and I saw Ma peering toward him, even though she attempted to be discreet. But my poor ma was never the discreet type."

"Did your pa buy the doll for her?"

"Did she find out her present?"

"Did you buy her something else?"

The questions came one after the other. "Yes, we did, but Pa pretended like we didn't. Ma loved that porcelain doll because she'd never owned one in her life. Her pa never allowed such frivolous things, even though he and my grandmother could well afford it." His smile faded and a flicker of something—sorrow, perhaps—claimed his countenance. He recovered and continued. "I'll never forget that day, just as you won't forget the day your pa received the crate full of toys and you got to try them first." He ruffled Frederick's hair. "I best let Miss Beauchamp start your lessons."

The children expressed their disapproval of trading time with the reverend with having to do book work, but took their seats and pulled out their slates.

"Sorry for the interruption," Reverend Solomon said.

"They enjoyed it and it started our day off well." *And it took my mind off any pending worries.*

"All right, then." A corner of his mouth lifted into a lopsided grin.

And a rush of heat rose in Lydie's face and neck. It must have been because of the warmth from the stove in the now-warm schoolhouse.

Surely not because she was softening to the handsome and personable Reverend Solomon.

CHAPTER SIXTEEN

SOLOMON SHOVED HIS HANDS in the pockets of his coat and lumbered through the snow toward the mercantile for the elder meeting. He found a hole in the pocket and curled his fingers in a tight ball to protect them from the cold air.

His time at the school created a pleasant diversion with the children's enthusiasm and the prompting of the memory from years ago. And lest he forget Miss Beauchamp with her pretty smile and the gratitude she expressed when he stacked the wood.

He would be remiss if he didn't admit to being drawn to her sweet personality. Solomon hoped to have a moment to tell her he was sorry for the prank. Yet again, no opportunity presented itself with Frederick's interruption and the subsequent conversation with the pupils.

This morning, he'd spent a fair amount of time in prayer for God's direction. And now it was clear to him what he should do. He would resign from being a reverend in Willow Falls. Next spring when the weather cleared, Solomon would decide where to go next. Perhaps South Pass City as he'd contemplated. Or maybe to the Montana Territory or even south to Texas.

Just not Minnesota.

Not back to Grandfather.

No matter what circumstances arose, he now knew he'd not return to the man who had disowned him.

In the meantime, Solomon would ask if he could board with Abe and assist him on the ranch. In the short amount of time he'd known him, Abe had become the grandfather Solomon always wished he'd had. What would life have been like after his parents' death if Abe had raised him?

At least Solomon had earned enough money to purchase a few hymnals. Perhaps Mr. Morton would order them and take over the duties of preaching until they found a new reverend.

Solomon passed the saloon, where even on a cold wintry day, men sat inside imbibing and wasting the precious life God had given them. He passed the post office and finally reached the mercantile. *Lord, if it is Your will that I relinquish my duties as a reverend, please make it clear. I seek only to do Your will.* He stared up at the graying sky. *And, Lord, will You please give me the opportunity to speak with Miss Beauchamp?*

He did his best to stand a little taller. If God's will was such that being a preacher in Willow Falls was not in His plan, then the Lord had a different plan. And if He had a different plan, He would take care of Solomon. Right?

Solomon gave his life to Christ as a young boy. Had walked with the Lord as best as he could, although he was far from perfect. Mistakes still marred him. But God was faithful and had brought him through many trials. Then why the doubt that lingered on the fringes of his mind? Why the worry that maybe, just maybe, God didn't have this situation under control?

He opened the door to the mercantile, stomped off the snow that clung to his boots, and entered. An aroma of cookies permeated the air. Had Mrs. Morton baked goodies for the meeting?

Solomon would miss the townsfolk he'd grown fond of: Abe, the Townsends, the Mortons, Doc and Mrs. Garrett, the students, and Miss Beauchamp.

Miss Beauchamp. Why did she keep finding her way into his thoughts?

"They're in the back room," said Mrs. Morton, who was arranging household items on the shelf. "There are cookies on the table. Help yourself." She smiled and gestured toward the back room.

Seconds later, Solomon sat in one of the chairs in the back room at Morton's Mercantile. His heart thrummed steadily in his chest and sweat beaded on his brow. He needed to tell the elders it was time for him to move on from Willow Falls. To find another flock to serve. *To show Grandfather he was right.*

He was the first one to arrive and he could hear conversations in the mercantile, most notably the voice of Mr. Morton. Doc walked in next and took a seat beside him and set his brown leather doctor's bag on the floor. "Never know when you might need it," he chuckled.

Solomon offered a weak smile. He would miss Doc and many of the residents of Willow Falls.

Sheriff Townsend took the seat on the other side of Doc. "Had a couple of disorderly conduct situations already today. I hope Willow Falls doesn't become like so many places in the Wyoming Territory."

Finally, Mr. Morton arrived, walking backwards into the room as he continued the remnants of his conversation with Mr. Castleberry.

They opened with prayer before Doc said, "Well, son, we have something we need to speak with you about."

The tightness in Solomon's shoulders was unrelenting, and he did his best to relax. "Yes, sir, but first, might I say a few words?"

Doc exchanged glances with Sheriff Townsend and Mr. Morton. "All right, then, son, you have something you need to tell us?" If Solomon hadn't been so anxious about the whole thing, he might have laughed at the continual way Doc called him "son," even though it would be a stretch for him to be old enough to be Solomon's father.

Solomon cleared his throat and took a deep breath. "Thank you, gentlemen, for allowing me to speak my piece." He had the men's rapt attention. Sheriff Townsend's brows formed parallel lines over the bridge of his nose. Mr. Morton leaned forward, and Doc steepled his fingers. "I am appreciative of you all giving me a chance here in Willow Falls."

Mr. Morton started to open his mouth, but closed it upon the shaking of Doc's head. "Best let him speak."

And speak he must or he'd lose all resolve. "I have come to love the beauty of this town with its mountains in the near distance and its crisp air. I consider you my friends and have formed other friendships as well." Sweat trickled down his back and he shifted in his seat. *Lord, please give me the words.* Hadn't he rehearsed what he would say several times this morning? Preparing every word to say, anticipating every thought he'd think while sharing his piece, and practicing his responses to the elders' vocal reactions? Then why the collywobbles?

"Anyhow," Solomon continued, "I reckon it's time to move on so Willow Falls can find another reverend. One who will bring more folks to church. One who will be more adept at teaching the Word of God." Even as he said the words, a pain hit him in the chest. Could he really say goodbye to this new town? Could he really allow Grandfather to be correct?

Solomon closed his eyes briefly and prayed for God's guidance. The men said nothing as awkward seconds ticked by. He picked at a nail and figured maybe he ought to say more. Maybe apologize for not being what they wanted him to be. He opened his mouth to say the words that needed to be said. But his voice collided with Sheriff Townsend's words.

"Reverend, would you give us a minute of privacy?"

"Yes, sure." Solomon rose and left the room. Standing on the boardwalk outside the mercantile, he saw Miss Beauchamp in the school yard, bundled in her coat and green scarf. The regret of their first meeting lingered in his mind. What if they had met under different circumstances? If she hadn't been the new teacher? Or if he hadn't been volunteered to monitor the prank tradition? What if he'd met her while traveling on the stagecoach or she was someone in town's daughter and he'd met her in church?

She wore a pale blue dress today, and as always, he found her to be a comely woman. But the maroon dress she wore that first day he'd met her was his favorite. It went well with her pretty eyes. He dutifully noted her amiable personality and her reputation for being kind, gracious, a good teacher, and a godly woman. None of these traits had escaped his notice. And she had a sweet laugh. Solomon had witnessed that a time or two. What would it have been like to be the one to make her laugh? To make her smile?

If onlies crowded his already frazzled mind. There was no guarantee she would have liked him even as a friend, but he couldn't help but wonder if he could have built upon the beginnings of the friendship he thought might have been possible after he found her brooch.

Regret consumed him.

One thing was certain. Miss Beauchamp's aunts would be gratified that the "brash young reverend" had left town come next spring.

Was it his imagination or did her gaze meet his? Solomon averted his attention to the bank across the street. He really ought to be less obvious.

"Son?" Doc asked. "You can come back now."

Solomon shook away his thoughts of Miss Beauchamp and wandered back to his place in the back room. Doc closed the door behind him. "We've had some time to discuss your resignation."

He held his breath. This moment would seal his future and if, out of extreme desperation, he did return to Grandfather, tail between his legs, as the saying went, God would be there with Him. "Yes, sir."

Sheriff Townsend stretched his legs out in front of his chair. "We respect what you're saying, Solomon…"

Solomon attempted not to think of how he'd miss the title "Reverend" for that was just plain prideful on his part.

"And we would like to ask you to please reconsider."

Solomon was about to stand, shake hands, and be on his way to pack up his meager belongings in the parsonage when his brain finally comprehended Sheriff Townsend's words. "Pardon me?"

The three men laughed, Doc's chortle being the loudest and most emphatic. "We said we'd like you to reconsider," he said.

"But with all respect, sirs, I have not been the kind of reverend you thought I'd be when you sent me the acceptance letter."

"And what kind of reverend did you figure we were in need of?" Mr. Morton asked.

Solomon thought about all he'd heard about Reverend Glenn. "Someone older, more experienced in life's occurrences. Someone who is able to fill the church with parishioners instead of drive them away."

"Hold the buggy," said Doc. "Did we say that's what we wanted?"

Mr. Morton scratched his head. "Don't recall saying that, not in those words anyhow."

"Someone like Reverend Glenn," Solomon blurted before he could rein in his tongue.

Doc nodded. "Reverend Glenn was a fine man. He cared deeply about the people in Willow Falls and was the first reverend we had before you came. He is missed. But he's not the only one who can preach and grow us in the knowledge of God's Word."

"But everyone attended church when he was here." Solomon thought of the praises he'd heard from the townsfolk about his predecessor. He'd fought a feeling of envy a time or two even though he'd never met the man.

"Not everyone," said Sheriff Townsend. "Not by a stretch. Willow Falls still has a good many folks who don't care about God or church. Reverend Glenn did have a gift for speaking well from the pulpit and, more importantly, he loved the Lord. But did he have every resident in Willow Falls filling the pews? Not at all."

Solomon grappled with the thoughts spinning through his mind. They wanted him to reconsider? They wanted him to *stay*? They weren't concerned he wasn't like Reverend Glenn? He wouldn't have to move on or even return to Grandfather and ask for his forgiveness for leaving the farm? He could live out the calling that pressed on his heart with such force he could scarcely ignore it? But what of his youth? "But I'm young and unmarried. I haven't experienced what an older preacher has."

"I recall when I first took the role of sheriff. I was grateful they gave me a chance."

"You were the only one who applied for the job," Mr. Morton said.

Sheriff Townsend tilted his head in a yes. "That may be, but I was only twenty-three, just two years older than the reverend. You could have decided Willow Falls would have been better off without a lawman."

"And have our town turn into another outlaw haven?" Doc asked. "Look at what's been happening to that new town, Poplar Springs."

"It helped a mighty bit that you apprehended that notorious outlaw two months in," added Mr. Morton.

Sheriff Townsend laughed. "Don't remind the missus of that. She'd rather forget that day."

Doc shook his head. "Took a great deal to put you back together after that. They didn't call that outlaw a sharpshooter for nothing."

Solomon watched the interaction among the men. The town was relatively new and the men hadn't known each other for an extended period of time, yet they'd grown in their friendship. Would that someday be how it would be for Solomon? Would he be a part of their camaraderie?

"We'd be much obliged if you'd stay," Sheriff Townsend said, and the others concurred.

"Course, this is all up to you," said Mr. Morton. "If you want to leave, we won't stop you, but we'd rather you stay."

"And not just because there are no other applicants." Doc tossed a knowing grin to Sheriff Townsend. "But because we see the potential in you and think you're already doing a fine job. And as far as the naysayers go, there will always be folks like that no matter where you go. You just keep serving the Lord the way you're doing and everything will fall into its rightful place."

Solomon's shoulders relaxed but his throat thickened. He was being given a second chance to proceed with where he believed God wanted him.

"You're probably wondering why we called this meeting," said Mr. Morton.

"I believed it was because you were going to suggest I resign."

Sheriff Townsend shook his head. "No, we were going to discuss the church's roof, which Doc said has a small leak, plus some other trivial issues, but no, we weren't going to talk about your resignation."

Solomon closed his slack jaw. Disbelief reigned in his mind. *They want me to stay? They wanted only to discuss a roof leak and other trivial issues?* How much time had he spent worrying about what *might* be the topic of conversation?

"Have you made a decision?" Mr. Morton asked, reaching for his third cookie.

"I'll stay." His words sounded like a croak in his own ears.

Doc stood and clapped him on the shoulder. "That's good news. Good news indeed." He snagged a cookie and took his seat again. "Now, we do need to mention the parishioners. Your idea for the potluck was, as my wife, said, 'extraordinary.' It brought folks together and reminded us all of what we love about this town. Perhaps in the summer we could have a few more of those."

"And Candace asked if we could have a harvest potluck as well. Seems folks raved about her mock turtle soup."

The conversation continued and Solomon, for the first time since moving to Willow Falls, finally felt like he belonged.

CHAPTER SEVENTEEN

SOLOMON STILL NEEDED TO apologize to Miss Beauchamp for the prank ordeal. Several times he'd tried, and several times he'd been interrupted. So, on a blustery fall evening, he strolled to the Castleberry home, hoping to have the courage to ask for Miss Beauchamp's forgiveness.

It wasn't so much the pranks he needed to discuss, but the irresponsibility on his part to reiterate to the pupils the rules of what the school board determined could very well become a tradition.

A gust of wind swirled the leaves and rain pelted him. Solomon ducked his head and forged on before he lost his resolve. Hopefully Frederick was not visiting the Castleberrys.

The whitewashed two-story home graced the corner of Main Street and First Street. It stood out from all of the other homes and reminded Solomon of some of the fancy houses in Minnesota when he visited the city.

Solomon stepped on the porch, rubbed his hands together, not only to stave off the cold that seeped through his thin coat, but also in nervousness of what was to come. Perhaps this wasn't the best idea. What if the words came out wrong or Miss Beauchamp wasn't willing to talk with him? What if Mrs. Castleberry didn't invite him in? She and her husband hadn't been to church and were rumored to be some of the naysayers against him preaching.

Not that Solomon was still heeding rumors about whether or not he was suitable for the position, not after his meeting with the elders.

"You're daft, boy. You should have apologized to the woman long ago." What Grandfather would say about the situation with Miss Beauchamp trickled into his mind.

Solomon pushed the thoughts aside. Grandfather wormed his way into far too many musings.

Mrs. Castleberry answered his knock. "Reverend Solomon, of what do we owe the pleasure?"

"Good evening, ma'am. I'm wondering if I might speak with Miss Beauchamp."

Mrs. Castleberry arched an eyebrow. "Very well, do come in. I'll see if she is taking callers."

Taken aback by both the woman's formality and candid words, Solomon stepped slowly into the home. A warm fire glowed in the fireplace and the aroma of something cooking—perhaps roast beef and potatoes—permeated the air. He inhaled and ignored the rumbling in his stomach.

Seconds ticked by until finally Miss Beauchamp walked down the stairs. Solomon clutched his hat in his hands and caught himself crimping the brim. He attempted to loosen his grip. His hands were clammy and he shifted his feet.

"Miss Beauchamp, I trust you have made Reverend Solomon Eliason's acquaintance?" Mrs. Castleberry asked.

"Yes, ma'am, I have."

"Very well. Reverend, please do join us in the parlor." Mrs. Castleberry led Miss Beauchamp and Solomon to an adjoining room that featured a settee and two chairs, along with an impressive bookcase, several paintings on the walls, and a rug on the floor. But what he noticed most was the piano against the far wall. His gaze lingered on it for a moment and a sense of nostalgia and melancholy washed over him.

Miss Beauchamp sat on one of the chairs, Mrs. Castleberry on the other, and Solomon planted himself on the settee, which seemed far too delicate and flowery for a man.

"Mr. Castleberry is still at the bank with his numbers. The company requires long hours of him, but he should be home directly. Please do commence with your conversation. Pay me no mind as I intend to continue my reading of *Sense and Sensibility*." Mrs. Castleberry opened her book and began to read.

Solomon caught himself bouncing his knee and struggled to rein in his nervousness. "Uh, Miss Beauchamp..." His eyes met hers and he realized again how lovely she was. Her hazel, almost brown, eyes held a softness in them, a kindness, that drew him. A wisp of her dark hair had escaped and rested on her cheek. She had folded her dainty hands in her lap. And she wore that maroon dress with the brooch.

Would she recall his assistance in helping her locate the brooch when she decided whether or not to forgive him?

Would she forgive him?

Or would Miss Beauchamp be like Grandfather and hold his transgression against him for the rest of his life?

Mrs. Castleberry peered over the top of her book. "Reverend Solomon, do tend to the matter at hand," she said.

Heat rushed up the back of his neck and Solomon wiped a clammy hand on his trousers. He'd been staring.

And caught while doing so.

Solomon removed his coat. Had it suddenly grown warmer in the room?

"Yes, ma'am. Uh, Miss Beauchamp, I came to—I came here to apologize." He glanced around the spacious room. Would Frederick emerge at any time and interrupt his words? Would the lad's ongoing diatribe prevent Solomon from saying the words that needed to be said? But the boy wasn't there, and Solomon expelled a sigh of relief. He cleared his throat and continued. "I came here to apologize for the pranks at the school."

Miss Beauchamp's eye again met his and he almost forgot how to breathe. What would she say in response?

"Mr., or rather, Reverend, I appreciate..."

Mrs. Castleberry again peered over her book, this time in Miss Beauchamp's direction. "Do speak louder, Lydie, I fear no one can hear that diminutive voice of yours."

"Oh!" Miss Beauchamp gasped and placed a hand to her mouth. Red colored her cheeks.

This was just as awkward for her as it was for him.

And Mrs. Castleberry, a high society lady, was not making the situation any easier.

"Reverend, I do appreciate you stopping by." She paused and averted her attention to Mrs. Castleberry, likely to see if the woman was going to again insert herself into the conversation. "Reverend, thank you for stopping by."

If nothing else transpired this evening, Miss Beauchamp had expressed her gratitude for his arrival at the Castleberry home.

"Well, then, I reckon..."

"I do appreciate..."

He paused when he realized they both spoke at once. "Please, go ahead," he deferred.

"Thank you, kindly."

Solomon edged forward on the settee so he could hear her more clearly. Was this the same woman who was chirping in the school that day while addressing her imaginary students? The same woman who sang the *Star-Spangled Banner* in a melodious voice?

He watched as she bit her lip. Would she continue speaking? Should he say his piece? Should he take his leave?

Sounds of someone in the kitchen clanging dishes temporarily drew him from his thoughts. Miss Beauchamp's voice drew him back.

"I do appreciate you stopping by to apologize."

"Yes, well, I'm not apologizing so much for the pranks..."

Her wide-eyed countenance told him he'd poorly chosen his words. "What I mean to say is that I am apologizing for the pranks, but mostly for the way it was handled." Phew. An entire sentence without stalling. "What I mean to say is that I was to have reiterated to the students the rules of the prank. I failed to do so. As a matter of fact, I forgot to do so. It was negligence and complete tomfoolery on my part, and for that, I do apologize. I was to have stopped them before they entered the school and..." now he was rambling. If Solomon hadn't heard it with his own ears, he'd know it by the expression on both Miss Beauchamp's and Mrs. Castleberry's faces.

"I forgive you, Reverend Solomon."

"And as such, I would like to seek your forgiveness for my lack of responsibility. I had every intention of stopping them on their way into the school. But I was preoccupied with a sermon I was supposed to write and then some other things that distracted me." *Like you, whom I thought was a student, reprimanding pupils and singing.*

"I forgive you."

"So if you could forgive me and perhaps..."

Mrs. Castleberry's firm, but respectful voice interrupted him. "She says she forgives you, Reverend. Do leave it at that. Goodness, but you are a verbose young man."

She forgave him? How had he missed her words? "You forgive me?"

"Yes."

Solomon swallowed hard. How could it be that a woman he barely knew forgave him for his error, but his own grandfather—his own flesh and blood—could neither forgive nor forget all of the transgressions he'd committed as a youngster?

Some of those had been minor transgressions such as returning home after school late because of a winter storm or forgetting to be sure the wood was stacked up to the mark Grandfather wrote on the wall during winter. And some had been major transgressions, like forgetting to shut the barn door or, more importantly, answering God's call to shepherd a flock in the Wyoming Territory.

"Reverend Solomon?" Miss Beauchamp's voice halted his dismal thoughts of his past mistakes.

"Yes, thank you, Miss Beauchamp. Thank you for your forgiveness." He heard his own voice crack. Would she notice it too and see it as a sign of weakness?

"You're a weak boy, Solomon. You should be able to carry more wood than that." Grandfather had stacked the pile of logs so high on Solomon's arms that he couldn't see over them. The weight had strained his young muscles to the point that they gave out and the logs thudded to the ground. For days afterwards, Grandfather made Solomon haul stacks of wood to the end of the road and back for several hours. Then he was reprimanded for not getting his chores done.

There had been no pleasing Grandfather.

"Now that that is settled..." Mrs. Castleberry was saying, "why don't the two of you reintroduce yourselves and start over?" She stood and placed her book on the chair. "Come along, Lydie."

Miss Beauchamp stood and Solomon did the same, his mind still contemplating Lydie's forgiveness. He knew he struggled with dwelling on things, but this was something he wanted to dwell on.

"As you both may or may not know, I was born and raised back East. I was born into a wealthy family and we were taught all of the social graces through numerous classes." Mrs. Castleberry appeared thoughtful. "When I married Mr. Castleberry, I imagined us residing near home. However, the bank transferred him to Denver. That was a change, but one I could endure. Then we were told we must move here to this uncivilized and barren town. Thankfully, our daughter was properly raised with all the conveniences and etiquette classes. Until she married a rancher and now resides in Nelsonville, but I digress. I feel it my duty to help young folks understand that just because we reside in the uncultured town of Willow Falls does not mean we forsake our duties to be proper." She paused. "Now, Reverend Solomon Eliason, I present to you Miss Lydie Beauchamp."

Lydie did a slight curtsy and Solomon nodded respectfully. Would Mrs. Castleberry instruct them further?

"Do start over in your acquaintance. Put the prank behind you." The woman's words resonated with Solomon. He could pretend this was the first time meeting Miss Beauchamp, as he had hoped to have met her under different circumstances.

"It's nice to meet you, Reverend."

"And you as well." The formality of his words almost caused him to chuckle. He sounded like a dandy.

Miss Beauchamp smiled at him and Solomon nearly forgot who he was and where he was. Finally, his memory returned. "Call me Solomon, if you'd like."

"Please and you may call me by my name. What I mean to say is that you may call me by my first name. You may call me Lydie."

Mrs. Castleberry let out an exaggerated sigh. "All right, now that formalities are over, would you care to stay for supper, Reverend?"

After supper, Lydie, Solomon, and the Castleberrys returned to the parlor. She watched as Solomon ambled toward the piano. He smoothed his hand along the fine wood of the ornate instrument, pausing on one of the ivories and gently pressing it.

"Do you play, Reverend Solomon?" Mrs. Castleberry asked.

"I do not, but my mother did."

A wistful expression, mixed with hurt, filled his eyes. Had he lost his ma as she had?

Mr. Castleberry stood beside Solomon, his smaller and thinner stature overwhelmed by Solomon's tall and muscular one. "That was an arduous undertaking to have that brought here," said Mr. Castleberry. "We had it shipped to Denver, which was not too terribly difficult. But bringing it here when we moved? Now that was tedious."

"And I have appreciated it many times over," added Mrs. Castleberry.

"Yes, my dear, so you have."

Lydie watched the interaction between the couple. They were of high society, something Lydie knew little about. Their home, so out of place in Willow Falls and likely the entire Wyoming Territory for that matter with the exception of the Symons home, was likely the only one within the Territory to boast a piano.

"Why don't you play for us, dear?" Mr. Castleberry asked.

"Certainly." As if she had awaited his invitation, Mrs. Castleberry stood immediately and sashayed to the instrument. "This is a rather new tune, only a few years old. My darling sister in New York sent me the music." Mrs. Castleberry pointed to the paper on the piano. "It's called *If You've Only Got a Moustache* and it was written by the esteemed Stephen Foster."

Mrs. Castleberry positioned herself on the round piano stool, glided her fingers along the ivories and played the tune, her head leaning forward and back and her eyes closed as she relished the tune. The tinkling of the keys sounded and she pressed her foot on the foot pedal.

Lydie had heard Mrs. Castleberry play thrice before in the evenings after supper. She was a gifted musician and mentioned she'd been trained by a distinguished pianist in New York as a young girl.

While the music was delightful, Lydie's attention focused on Solomon. He had closed his eyes, an undecipherable visage lining his features.

When she finished, Mrs. Castleberry took a bow. "Now tell me, Reverend, did your mother play often?"

Solomon nodded. "She did. She was a gifted pianist, just as you are, ma'am. She played mostly hymns and oftentimes blessed us with her music during church services."

"Well, one could hardly expect to see a piano in the church in Willow Falls," guffawed Mrs. Castleberry and Mr. Castleberry concurred.

Solomon's expression dulled and a wistful countenance overcame him. Did he wish for a piano to be in the church in Willow Falls? Was he missing his ma? Lydie understood what it was like to miss someone, both those who had passed and those who lived but were far away.

The conversation turned to other items and the piano incident was forgotten. But Lydie wondered if there was more to Reverend Solomon Eliason than one would surmise.

That evening, Lydie pulled the covers up to her shoulders and stared at the ceiling. The full moon shone through the curtains, but the room was otherwise dark. She rehashed the events of the evening over and over in her mind. She had sounded like such a flibbertigibbet. And if the brown-and-yellow rug could have swallowed her up, she would have welcomed it.

What must Reverend Solomon think of her? *"Please and you may call me by my name. What I mean to say is that you may call me by my first name. You may call me Lydie."* Could she have sounded any more like a ninny?

Her cheeks burned with embarrassment. She pulled the pillow out from under her head and placed it over her face for a brief moment, hoping to drown out the memory of the night's events. Lydie replaced the pillow back beneath her head and again stared at the ceiling. The house was quiet with the exception of her random sighs.

Had the reverend, or Solomon, as she now called him, thought her obtuse when she offered her forgiveness so quickly? He hadn't responded, only stood there, his handsome face taking on a troubled expression. Did he think she was untruthful?

And why did she care about what he thought? For wasn't it just recently she found Solomon to be a brash and insolent cad? Why the sudden change in opinion of him?

Of course, she had softened to him in recent days after watching his interaction with the children and listening to his sermons.

Lydie recalled his dapper appearance as he sat on the settee. But she also recalled his humility in apologizing. That drew her to him. He was nothing like Mr. Wilkins who couldn't even apologize for breaking Aunt Fern's heart. Such a hateful man.

No, Solomon was nothing like Mr. Wilkins.

He'd preached a good sermon the times she'd heard him speak. As though he cared deeply for the people to whom he spoke. A bit nervous behind the podium and he did tend to be a wordy sort, but Lydie could see Solomon loved the Lord.

He did seem forthright and sincere when he said he was sorry for failing to discuss the pranks more fully with the students.

So maybe Lydie could see him in a new way now that Solomon had apologized, she had forgiven him, and they had started over in making their acquaintance.

The memory of the first day of school lingered on the edges of her mind. The sleeping children, the rambunctious children, the disobeying, and the fear that she was not qualified for the position.

But now here she was a few months later, settling into her role as a teacher in Willow Falls. Yes, she could forgive Solomon, and if she was honest, some of the prank was actually humorous. For instance, how had the pupils been so convincing in their sleep? She let out a small giggle. The singing of several different songs and their off-key voices was hideous. Perhaps she ought to instruct them in harmonizing.

Lydie rose, lit the lamp, and reached for her stationery. Today seemed to be a monumental day, one that needed to be recorded in a letter to the aunts. Wouldn't they be surprised and perhaps elated to know she was now settling into her new life? Maybe they would worry less.

She envisioned Aunt Myrtle's and Aunt Fern's facial expressions when they heard about Solomon. They taught her the importance of forgiveness at a young age and lived the example in their own lives.

Dearest Aunt Myrtle and Aunt Fern,

Reverend Solomon stacked wood at the school the other day and made sure the fire was lit before the students and I arrived. Such a kind gesture was well-received and appreciated. He is a chatty sort and spent a fair amount of time with the students reminiscing about a delightful story from his past. He has a way with children and they do adore him.

I forgot to mention I spent some time with Mrs. Castleberry and Mrs. Symons last week. Unfortunately, my mouth did get the better of me when Mrs. Symons reverted to saying unkind things about the reverend. While I did find him to be a brash and insolent cad after the pranks, I find him a little less so now. I haven't heard anything more from Mrs. Symons, and after a brief chat with Mrs. Castleberry, all seems to be well.

Lest you believe the story stops there, Reverend Solomon arrived at the house tonight and apologized after all this time for the pranks. Why he took so long, I truly have no idea, but as you always say, Aunt Fern, "it is better to be late than to not be at all."

Mrs. Castleberry, bless her heart, did add to an already awkward situation. But in the end, all was well.

Solomon, as I now call him, offered his apology and I forgave him. He seemed sincere and I do believe he is sorry for his actions. As such, we have been reacquainted, thanks to Mrs. Castleberry, who makes it a point to uphold social graces. She is a nice woman and I appreciate her gracious hospitality, although she is a bit of a busybody.

Today was a juncture for Solomon and me, and I believe we shall be friends henceforth.

Perhaps he is not as impudent as I once thought him to be. After all, Solomon is a man of God and cares for others. The students adore him and he works hard, not only as a preacher, but doing other jobs. I've seen him assisting Mr. Morton numerous times, and someone mentioned he works for Mr. Pinson when not otherwise occupied with writing sermons or visiting the sick.

I love and miss you both terribly and wish we could visit in person about these latest developments.

Please write and let me know how you both fare. Is Mr. Peabody still being ornery? How is Mrs. Peabody?

With Love,

Lydie

As she re-read the letter, a thought crossed her mind.

Her words made it sound as though she was fond of Solomon. Lydie reached for a fresh sheet of paper. She couldn't have the aunts thinking such things. Perhaps she should start over and re-write the letter.

Lydie sat, pencil suspended in air. But then again, would it be so bad that her aunts thought her fond of Solomon?

For perhaps she was growing fond of him. Just the slightest bit.

CHAPTER EIGHTEEN

SOLOMON STOOD AT THE door after services concluded to shake hands with the congregants. Lydie noticed that today both Richard's and Alice's families attended. Slowly, the humble church in Willow Falls was growing. She invited the Castleberrys last week and hoped they would soon attend as well.

"That was a laudable sermon, Solomon."

"Thank you, Lydie." A glint touched his eyes and she hoped the compliment encouraged him as she intended. Seconds ticked by and for a moment, all other activity inside and outside of the church ceased to exist. Had she ever noticed what a fine man he was? Now that Lydie knew his honest error in the pranks, she'd come to see him in a different way.

As a considerate and caring man with a benevolent heart and a desire to do the Lord's work. A handsome man with strong and rugged features and a smile that made her heart stutter.

"Might I accompany you to the Castleberry home?"

"Certainly."

Solomon closed the door of the church and offered his elbow. Lydie placed her hand through the crook of his arm and together they traipsed through the snow to the Castleberry home at the edge of town. The day was cold, but bright and sunny, and the sunshine caused the snow to sparkle as though diamonds embedded themselves in the white fluff. She reveled in their time together as they shared in pleasant conversation.

They reached the Castleberry home all too soon, but she wasn't ready for their time to end.

She needn't have worried.

Mrs. Castleberry immediately invited them both inside. "You musn't stay outside too long or you'll catch your death of cold. Reverend Solomon, do stay for the noonday meal, won't you?"

The woman possessed a dramatic flair that would have served her well had she joined the theater. In her lovely dress, complete with a strand of pearls, she belonged more so in a large city with all its fineries than in the uncultivated Wyoming Territory.

"Thank you, Mrs. Castleberry. I will do that." Solomon followed Lydie into the house.

"There are freshly made sugar biscuits while we wait for the meal to be prepared. Please, Lydie and Reverend, do make yourselves comfortable. I'll be back momentarily."

Lydie's mouth watered at the thought of the delicacy made to perfection by the woman who prepared all of the desserts and many of the main meals for the Castleberrys.

Moments later, they returned to the parlor and ate the scrumptious sugar biscuits topped with a thin glaze. Mrs. Castleberry took her place with sewing in hand. Mr. Castleberry seated himself by the fireplace and perused a newspaper.

Lydie perched on the other chair and Solomon sat on the settee.

"Good afternoon, Lydie and Reverend." Mr. Castleberry peered above the newspaper, his glasses perched on his nose.

"Good afternoon, sir. I see you're reading a newspaper."

Mr. Castleberry nodded. "Yes, although it's not current news as I receive it from my brother back East, but it's better to read about news late than read about it never."

"I'm quite fond of the news myself," Solomon said.

And Lydie added the fact that he was an intelligent young man to the things she was growing fond of about him.

"While I do enjoy reading about our new president, I find myself quite appreciating the news about the new Cincinnati Red Stockings. I played some baseball myself back in the day." He patted his rotund stomach and Mrs. Castleberry laughed.

"Yes, back in the day, dear."

Mr. Castleberry sat up straighter in his chair. "As a member of an amateur men's baseball club in our city, I often participated in the pastime."

"Indeed. He still talks about it after all these years."

An hour later, Lydie and Solomon joined the Castleberrys for the noonday meal. The serving of ham reminded Lydie Thanksgiving was next week. She wanted more than anything to spend it with Aunt Myrtle and Aunt Fern. Even eating Aunt Myrtle's burned dinner rolls and charred turkey would be a welcome reprieve to her homesickness.

Mr. and Mrs. Castleberry offered for her to attend Thanksgiving supper with them, and Lydie was grateful for such an invitation, but she'd rather not intrude on their time, especially since their daughter and her husband were arriving from Nelsonville.

A melancholy settled over her as she swirled her potatoes on her plate without taking a bite.

The older couple proceeded to discuss a variety of topics and Solomon leaned toward her, his breath tickling her ear. "Is everything all right, Lydie?"

"I was just deep in thought about Thanksgiving."

"Hard to believe it's next week."

Hard to believe indeed. She'd already been teaching in Willow Falls over two months. She watched as Solomon buttered his roll. Did he have somewhere to go for Thanksgiving? Did he miss his family? There was so little she knew about him and she realized she'd like to know more. Should she ask Mrs. Castleberry if Solomon could partake in their Thanksgiving meal as well? Were they growing more accustomed to him and therefore more open to attending church?

Questions crowded her mind.

"You have a lot on your mind this afternoon." Solomon's gaze held hers. The Castleberrys continued in their lively conversation.

"I was just thinking of how much I'm going to miss my aunts at Thanksgiving. Christmas will be all the more difficult."

"Ah, yes, the aunts." A smirk lined Solomon's dapper features and a slight dimple appeared in his chin.

"We're going to recline in the parlor. Do take your time to eat," Mrs. Castleberry said.

Mr. Castleberry pulled the chair out for his wife. "I'll be back momentarily for some dessert."

"Yes, likely soon," chortled Mrs. Castleberry as she and Mr. Castleberry disappeared to the parlor.

"It will be my first Thanksgiving away from them. I do appreciate the Castleberry's hospitality in inviting me to eat with them, but it won't be the same." She paused. "Do forgive me, Solomon. You likely have no place to go as well. Do you miss your family?" Guilt washed over her for being so preoccupied with her own disappointment.

"My parents died when I was ten. Holidays can be difficult as I miss them a lot. They were taken far too soon by the influenza, but over time, I've come to realize there are a good many charitable folks willing to allow this at-times too-verbose reverend to dine at their table."

While Solomon might think himself too verbose, Lydie appreciated conversation with him with his deep, yet calm, voice. "I'm sorry about your parents. Mine died as well when I was three. That's when the aunts took me in and raised me. They're my pa's older sisters." She thought of Aunt Myrtle and Aunt Fern and their graciousness in providing for her over the years. "Did you stay with a relative or did you go to an orphanage?"

His forehead creased and sadness overcame his expression. Lydie wished she hadn't asked. "I'm sorry, that was far too nosy of me."

"No, Lydie, it's...I was sent to live with my grandfather. It was him or the orphanage. I knew he wasn't a considerate man and that he only wanted me because he needed help on the farm. But still, I hoped he would come to love me. That I could make myself worthy of his love."

Her heart broke at his words. She'd had a wonderful upbringing with two compassionate relatives. Life hadn't been easy at times, but love abounded. To not know that kind of love... "Oh, Solomon, I am so sorry about your grandfather. First losing your parents, then being sent to live with a harsh man." Yet, he was such a tender soul with consideration for others. "Is he still alive?"

"He is. He still lives on the farm. When I mentioned about God's calling on my life to become a reverend, he told me if I left to never return. That it would be as if he never knew me." Solomon released a heavy sigh. "I really contemplated whether or not to leave. My parents and I were close and since they were gone, Grandfather was the only other family I had. Ultimately,

I left with only a few possessions: my horse, Bible, and a few clothes. But maybe God wasn't calling me to preach. Maybe it was just something I wanted." He pushed his empty plate slightly away from him. "I'm sorry for sharing this burden with you."

"Yoo-hoo, you two can come to the parlor whenever you're finished," called Mrs. Castleberry.

Lydie shared a knowing glance with Solomon. "We'll be right there, Mrs. Castleberry. Thank you, Solomon, for sharing that with me. I never knew. And, I, for one, am glad you decided to become a reverend. You have a gift for sharing the Word of God and the sooner people realize that and give you a chance, the better."

A corner of his mouth lifted. "I'm glad I came here too. At first, I thought about the Montana Territory or even south to Texas. Or even to South Pass City." He held her gaze for a moment and her heart threatened to stop beating.

Finally, after she'd gathered herself, she spoke again. "I suppose we should retreat to the parlor lest Mrs. Castleberry worry."

"I can't speak for Christmas, but Sheriff Townsend invited me to Thanksgiving supper at their house. Would you care to attend with me?"

"If you're sure the Townsends would be amenable to that."

"I'm sure they would be. Mrs. Townsend loves to bake and I think she misses her family as well."

Lydie's heart felt lighter. While partaking in Thanksgiving supper with Solomon and the Townsends wasn't the same as spending the holiday with the aunts, she wouldn't be spending it alone.

Solomon pulled the chair out for her and offered his hand to assist her from the table. The mere touch sent a warming shiver through her and she turned her head away from him lest he see the flush she knew was creeping up her face.

CHAPTER NINETEEN

SOLOMON AWOKE WITH A start. It was a fantastic idea, he just needed to implement it.

And wouldn't Lydie be surprised?

He worked on his sermon for Sunday, including underlining more passages in his new Bible, visited a sick parishioner, assisted Abe with a job, then returned to town to accomplish his plan.

The snow had fallen periodically throughout the day in soft fluttering flakes. Solomon waited outside the school, perched behind the left-hand side corner just in case Lydie emerged with the students.

"Psst..." he whispered to the first student.

Before long, all of the students stood with him around the corner of the school. "Is Miss Beauchamp still inside?"

"Yes, but she mentioned she'd be leaving soon," said Alice.

Solomon needed at least five minutes to discuss his plan. "Frederick, would you mind delaying Miss Beauchamp? I'll talk with you later at the mercantile."

As if he'd been given an all-important assignment, Frederick puffed out his chest and nodded. "Yes, sir, Reverend. I'm just the one for the job."

Frederick was just the one for the job all right. Poor Lydie.

When the youngster scampered up the stairs and back into the schoolhouse, Solomon quickly addressed the students. Thankfully, it wasn't cold today, but he'd be efficient anyhow. "I have an idea for a surprise for Miss Beauchamp."

"Are you fond of Miss Beauchamp?" Alice asked.

Solomon knew his facial expression likely gave away his true feelings. But he avoided the question and instead focused on his plan. "Next week is Thanksgiving, and Christmas will soon be here."

The children began to cheer, and Solomon held a finger to his mouth. "Shh. We don't want Miss Beauchamp to know we're having this meeting."

After they had quieted, he continued. "How would you like to be part of a Christmas choir?"

The response of their chorused voices indicated their excitement to join an ensemble. "How can we do that, Reverend Solomon?" Richard asked.

"Well, we'll need to practice. A couple of days a week after school beginning the Monday after Thanksgiving. But Miss Beauchamp can't know. It must remain a secret. Can everyone here keep a secret?"

Richard fidgeted, tugging on the sleeve of his coat. "I think I can. I hope I can."

The youngster's dubious mannerisms elicited some concern. "You would have to keep the promise not to tell her," he gently prodded.

"You can't tell her at all," admonished his older sister.

"All right. I won't tell." Richard reached up and pretended to button his lip. "It's a secret."

Satisfied Richard could be trusted, Solomon continued. "We'll put on a special performance by singing three or four songs.

Then we'll have cookies and hot chocolate. I was thinking we would have it at the mercantile since that's the largest place in town. We would invite parents, friends, and the entire town. But it would be a special concert for Miss Beauchamp to make her Christmas even more special."

He thought of her face when she'd told him how homesick she was and how difficult Thanksgiving and Christmas would be for her away from her aunts. If Solomon could help remedy some of that loneliness, it would be an achievement.

"When do we start?"

"Which songs will we sing?"

"My ma can bring her special Christmas cookies."

"What if Miss Beauchamp finds out and it wasn't Richard who told her? What if I did it, but accidentally?"

The questions continued until Solomon reminded them they must keep the noise down lest Miss Beauchamp become suspicious and wander outside. He gave them details on their first choir practice then watched as they traipsed through the snow, excited expressions on their faces and enthusiasm in their voices.

It had been a good, but tiring, day. Lydie's feet ached and she wanted nothing more than to rest in the chair in her bedroom at the Castleberry home and pen a letter to the aunts. She scooped up her belongings, fastened her coat, wrapped her scarf around her neck, and proceeded to leave the schoolhouse.

Noises of her boisterous pupils as they left school filled the air. She started toward the door when Frederick came bustling back inside. "Hello, Miss Beauchamp."

"Frederick, did you forget something?"

"No, ma'am. Just thought I'd talk with you for a bit."

Frederick could talk for more than "a bit" as he most certainly had the gift of conversation. Lydie ignored the weariness tugging on her and instead gave Frederick her full attention. "Is something wrong, Frederick?"

The youngster plopped in his seat and leaned back. "I've been thinking more and more about my future as a stagecoach driver."

Lydie wondered why this conversation couldn't have waited until another day when she wasn't exhausted. But she didn't say as much.

Frederick continued his diatribe. "You see, when them outlaws come and try to steal the money, I have a plan. I'm going to have a bag of fool's gold. It'll be closed and all so they can't see what's inside. I'll surrender it to them after a short fight. Not a fight that would put any lives in danger. No, ma'am. Just a bit of arguing and insisting they go their own way. Then when they threaten, I'll put my hands in the air and tell them..." he paused and changed the tone of his voice to a higher, frantic pitch. "Just take the gold. Please, take it. Just don't hurt my passengers!" He took a deep breath, but showed no signs of stopping. "They'll ride off to their hideout before they even realize they've been duped. What do you think, Miss Beauchamp? Pa says I have to be older to be a stagecoach driver, but I'm fixin' to start when I'm fourteen. Do you think that's old enough? Do you think they'll hire me?"

Goodness, if the boy wasn't loquacious! "That's an ambitious plan, Frederick."

"Yes, ma'am, it is." Frederick tapped on his chin with his finger thoughtfully. "I know how to drive a wagon. I've practiced plenty. You've ridden a stagecoach before—was it a thrilling ride?" His eyes enlarged to round saucers.

Lydie thought back to the journey from Minnesota and then the journey from Prune Creek to Willow Falls. *Thrilling* was not a term she would use to describe it. "It's a rough ride and the stagecoach sways to and fro. Your legs feel like they are on pins and needles when you finally disembark. We had several passengers this last ride and it was crowded to say the least." Her words were barely spoken before Frederick continued.

"Well, as Pa would say, 'not every job can be the best job'."

Lydie stifled a yawn. "Frederick, do you mind if we talk about this tomorrow?"

"Not at all, ma'am."

When Lydie attempted to gather her belongings once again and walk toward the door, Frederick leaped out of his chair in the most expedient manner in which she'd ever seen him move. "Just a minute, Miss Beauchamp." He sprinted toward the door, flung it open, stuck his head outside, and then returned to stand beside her.

"Is something wrong?" Lydie asked.

"No, ma'am, not at all. Just seeing to things."

Lydie was about to ask him if he could elaborate when he darted out the door. "See you tomorrow!"

Chapter Twenty

THE DAY BEFORE THANKSGIVING, Solomon rode his horse outside of town. Winter had begun its relentless reign over the area. This would be his first Wyoming Territory winter. Thankfully, the pile of logs outside the parsonage would see him through.

The area gave testimony to an artistic Creator with a variety of covered pines and a pond all resting in the shadow of the spectacular snow-tipped mountains in the near distance. He sucked in a breath and surveyed the expanse of acreage. With the exception of a neglected cabin, the property was idyllic.

He'd wandered out to the land thrice before but had never gone inside the house. The weathered cabin needed extensive repairs.

Solomon scanned the entire area. He would someday own the house and piece of land on which it sat.

He tethered his horse and walked to the front door of the cabin. An old wagon wheel covered with a few inches of snow leaned against a broken railing. A hole in the window invited creatures to visit, and the roof could use a good fixing. Curiosity bested him and he turned the rusted doorknob and entered.

Cobwebs shimmered in the light coming through the window. A rock fireplace filled with blackened logs invited him to imagine what it would be like in the winter with a roaring fire. A well-worn table with a tin plate and a chair missing one of the slats were the only furniture, and a tattered and faded curtain blew in the breeze.

He inspected the cabin more closely. While many repairs were needed, the home boasted a solid structure. Solomon wandered up the stairs, careful not to invite a splinter while holding on to the rough railing. Two stairs were missing and he cautiously stepped over them.

The upstairs boasted an additional area that could be divided into two rooms. He stared over the railing and into the lower level of the cabin. There was a great deal of work to be done, but he also saw potential.

Who had lived here and why had they left?

Solomon retreated several minutes later, the cabin still on his mind. "Lord, if it's Your will…" he said aloud, his voice the only noise besides the chirping of a random robin and the whistling of wind through the trees.

A plan formed in his mind and he prayed for guidance on how to proceed.

Willow Falls Bank stood directly across from the mercantile and was the only building exhibiting a brick front. His heart pounded as he stepped inside and he breathed one more prayer seeking wisdom.

"Hello, Reverend. What brings you to the bank?" Mr. Castleberry adjusted his spectacles and stepped from behind the barred teller window. He extended his hand.

"Hello, sir. I'm here to ask about the cabin near the pond just outside of town."

"The old Foss place?"

Solomon shrugged. "Not sure who owns it. It's weathered with a broken window."

"Ah, yes, the Foss place. What would you like to know about it?"

"Just about everything. Is it for sale?"

Mr. Castleberry walked to a shelf and opened the ledger. "It is. Mr. Foss arrived here just after I did. He procured a loan for the property and commenced to building the house on the land with the hopes his fiancée would join him here. Unfortunately, his fiancée decided neither the Wild West *nor* Mr. Foss were what she had in mind for her future. Mr. Foss defaulted on his loan, the bank foreclosed on the property, and Mr. Foss left the area. Someone said they heard he went to Virginia City in the Montana Territory. Not sure if that's true or not. All I knew was that my bank was burdened with an outstanding loan and a property no one wanted."

But Solomon wanted it. Wanted to put down roots in this town, especially after his meeting with the elders.

Lydie's face flashed in his mind.

And maybe, just maybe, start a life with a woman who'd been in his thoughts almost nonstop lately.

"I'm interested in purchasing it." Was he engaging in tomfoolery over his decision to buy the ranch?

Mr. Castleberry quirked an eyebrow. "It's good ranch land, but you don't make much being a reverend. Could you afford the payments?"

Not with his income now, but if he continued to work other jobs and was frugal... "What is the price?"

"Prices are typically $1.25 per unimproved acre and $3 to $5 per improved acre. This is good ranch land, but Mr. Foss hadn't time to do much improving. There's no barn and the house...are you sure you want to undertake the repairs something in such a dilapidated state would entail?"

"Yes, sir, I'm sure."

"All right, well, I would only ask for what was owed on it. There is interest from Mr. Foss's loan, but..." Mr. Castleberry paused and tilted his head. "I'll tell you what. I'll drop the interest owed from Mr. Foss and I'll charge you the unimproved-per-acre price."

Solomon was overwhelmed with gratitude. He extended his hand. "Thank you, Mr. Castleberry. Thank you so much. You won't be disappointed. I'll work really hard to improve the place and I won't let you down on the payments on the bank note." Grandfather's voice reminding him he'd never amount to anything threatened to surge to the forefront of his mind. With effort, Solomon shoved it aside. He *would* be successful in restoring the cabin. He *would* improve upon the land. And he *wouldn't* miss one payment.

Mr. Castleberry chuckled. "Well, I can see you're eager to set down roots and start life on your own ranch."

"That I am. I figure I can build a barn, get a few head of cattle, and have a chicken coop for starters. Nothing big, just enough to supplement my income." His calling in life would be, first and foremost, preaching.

"I'll ready the paperwork. Or if you'd like, we can wait until spring when you're able to begin working on the cabin."

Solomon gave it some thought. It would make more sense to stay in the parsonage through the winter, and besides, he couldn't do much in the way of repairs with the winter weather. "Much obliged, Mr. Castleberry. Thank you."

"Lydie invited the missus and me to church recently." He stroked his graying beard. "As you know, we only attended that first time you preached, but we didn't return."

Solomon wasn't sure he wanted to hear what Mr. Castleberry had to say. With God's help and the encouragement of the elders, he'd tried hard to put aside the notion that he was too young and too inexperienced to preach.

"I'm sorry I passed judgment on you. The missus and I favored Reverend Glenn's style of preaching and his extensive knowledge of the Bible. My wife, especially, was fond of Reverend Glenn as he reminded her of her father, whom she lost several years ago. When Reverend Glenn left, we weren't willing to give you a chance. For that I apologize." A fixed look of concentration crossed his face. "I aim to change that. We'll be there on Sunday and you have our full support."

Solomon's jaw went slack. Mr. Castleberry was apologizing? He and Mrs. Castleberry would be attending on Sunday? Lydie had invited them? "Thank you, sir. I appreciate that."

"Yes, well, we were planning to be in attendance on Sunday, but since you're here, I figured I might as well apologize." He briefly stared out the window before returning his gaze to Solomon. "I know somewhat the predicament you are in. You see, I was a banker in Denver for many years after we moved from back East. An eager young man came to work for the bank and they decided he was better suited for the position I currently held. Suffice it to say, the only available location for me if I wished to remain a bank employee was to move to Willow Falls. Mrs. Castleberry was plaintive about moving here. But thankfully, she has found a place amongst the townsfolk." Mr.

Castleberry lowered his voice. "Between you and me, I wish she'd find friends other than Mrs. Symons. But don't let on I said so."

Solomon left the bank with a new hope regarding the future. He and Mr. Castleberry had talked for several more minutes. The banker reassured him that if anyone else expressed interest in the Foss place that he would notify them it was sold.

And spring couldn't come soon enough for Solomon.

He tucked his hands in his pockets and started toward the parsonage. He would retrieve Lydie tomorrow afternoon at four o'clock and together they would attend Thanksgiving at the Townsend home.

As he neared the church, Solomon saw Lydie as she stood watching the children at recess. The wind blew her dark hair, spinning strands of it. The children played blindman's bluff, spinning a blindfolded student in a circle, then tromping through the snow in an attempt to escape from his grasp as they called out to him. Giggles filled the air.

"I remember this game," he said as drew next to her.

Lydie rewarded him with a smile. "It's one of their favorites and it doesn't matter if it's warm outside or freezing, they still all want to partake in it. Thankfully, they're all dressed warmly. As a matter of fact, it takes a while for them to remove all of their coats, scarves, hats, and gloves before we can resume class."

The children continued with their game, but he struggled to maintain his focus on anything but her. When had he come to have feelings for her? When had she come to be more than Miss Beauchamp, the teacher at the Willow Falls school?

A frigid wind blew, freezing the tips of his ears. Lydie shivered. He removed his coat and handed it to her.

"Are you sure? I don't want you to be cold." The caring expression endeared her all the more to him.

Ma's words reminding him to always be a gentleman entered his mind. "I'm fine. This shirt is plenty warm."

"If you're sure."

He hoped his smile convinced her. "I'm sure."

Lydie pulled on the coat. The sleeves flapped due to their length and they both laughed, their voices melding together in perfect harmony. "It's a mite bit big," he said as he assisted her in rolling up the sleeves.

And on that day, November 24, 1869, he began to fall in love with Lydie Beauchamp.

Chapter Twenty-One

THE WIND WHISTLED THROUGH the trees as Lydie and Solomon walked to the Townsend home.

My, but she was growing fond of him! Fond of his gentle way with those in need; fond of his extensive knowledge of the Bible; and fond of his marvelous sense of humor. The wind blew his light brown hair, giving him an even more rugged look. He smiled at her as they walked and her heart stuttered.

Candace ushered them inside the Townsend home a few minutes later. The aroma of turkey cooking in the oven mixed with the delectable scent of pumpkin pie filled the air. "Do come in and sit down. Supper is about to be served." She juggled the baby on her hip.

Lydie removed her coat and hung it on the nail near the door. "Can I help you prepare?"

"Yes, if you wouldn't mind setting the table." Candace handed the baby to Sheriff Townsend who stood near the fireplace visiting with Solomon.

After Sheriff Townsend said grace, they proceeded to eat. "Did you hear they apprehended the wanted outlaw gang in Nelsonville?"

"That's good to hear," said Solomon.

"Yes. Seems they caused all sorts of problems for ranchers when they broke into barns and stole everything from horses to small farm implements. They robbed nearly a dozen stagecoaches and shot at least two people, one who died. Glad they've been captured. We don't need the likes of them in Willow Falls."

Lydie shivered. What if they had started their stealing spree in this town instead of Nelsonville?

"Didn't you say Poplar Springs has become somewhat of a haven for outlaws?" Solomon asked.

Sheriff Townsend nodded. "I did. New town, but already there's more saloons than houses." He and Solomon continued in conversation on the topic of cattle rustling, horse theft, assault, Indian raids, and shootouts in the streets.

"Do you ever get scared living behind the jail?" Lydie asked Candace.

Candace snuggled the baby and held him close. "I did at first. I knew when I married a lawman life wouldn't be easy. There have been so many instances when Walker has had to leave Willow Falls to assist in tracking an outlaw. It's those times that are the most frightening, especially if there's a prisoner in the jail. But God has had His protective hand over both Walker and me, and for that I am grateful."

"Reckon I best take our prisoner some supper," said Sheriff Townsend. "Unfortunately, those who have no respect for the law don't stop their lawless ways just because it's a holiday."

Solomon joined Sheriff Townsend and Lydie assisted Candace in washing the dishes. "If there's extra, might I take some to Mr. and Mrs. Hurley? He's in ill health."

"What a grand idea! Yes, I'll prepare two plates for them. Perhaps on your way home, you and Solomon can deliver the food."

An hour later, Lydie carried one plate and Solomon the other and they walked to a house not far from the Townsend home to deliver the meal to the Hurleys.

"I enjoyed the evening," Solomon said when they reached the Castleberry's house sometime later.

"I did as well."

They stood for a brief moment, their gazes locked. After Solomon bid her goodbye, Lydie realized something profound.

On that day, Thursday, November 25, 1869, she began to fall in love with Solomon Eliason.

CHAPTER TWENTY-TWO

SNOWCAPPED MOUNTAINS, MIXED WITH a blue hue and the gentle breeze stirring the pines, reminded Solomon Christmas was on its way.

And he still had a few more ideas to make this year extra special for Lydie.

Solomon tromped through the snow and onto the porch of Doc's house. He lived close to town not far from the unpretentious building where he hung his shingle. Doc answered the door after the first knock.

"Reverend, is everything okay?" Even as he spoke, Doc buttoned his coat.

"Yes, everything is fine, I just have a favor to ask."

Doc moved aside, gestured him into the house while unbuttoning his coat, and placed it back on the hook by the door. Mrs. Garrett sat near the fireplace mending. "What a nice surprise, Reverend Solomon. What brings you here on this wintry day?"

Solomon noticed the plentiful stack of logs near the fireplace, but did his best to gather the courage to ask his question. "If I haul some wood into the house for you, might I borrow your sleigh for an hour?"

Doc reached for his coat once again. "Much obliged about your offer on the logs, but I just hauled several loads in earlier today."

Solomon's shoulders briefly slumped and he, with effort, once again stood tall. He'd have to think of another idea for Lydie.

"But," said Doc, "You may borrow the sleigh, but only for an hour. I'd say take it for the day, but I never know when someone might need my help. And if I'm called out to the backwoods, it's a lot easier with the sleigh."

Relief escaped his lips. "That would be fine, sir, I'd only need it for an hour. I would never want to prevent you from giving care to someone who needs it."

Doc patted Solomon on the back. "I know you wouldn't, son. You're a good man. Now, let's go out and hitch up the horses."

"Are you by chance taking a young lady on a sleigh ride?" Mrs. Garrett's green eyes twinkled.

Heat traveled in a slow wave up the back of Solomon's neck. "Uh, yes, ma'am."

"And would it be that lovely teacher, Miss Beauchamp?"

Solomon hadn't known Mrs. Garrett to be so ornery. "Yes, that's who it is."

"Just as I suspected." The woman rose and set her mending on the rocking chair. "Might I make some hot chocolate for you to take with you?"

Hot chocolate? That would make the event even more special. "Yes, Mrs. Garrett, that would be a mighty fine gesture."

A grin sprang across the woman's face as she toddled to the stove. "Give me just a few minutes and I'll have this in a pitcher and ready to go. Doc, do you have a crate we could use?"

Doc Garrett finished buttoning his coat. "I'll find one in the barn, dear," he said, likely accustomed to locating items for his wife.

"Now, Solomon. I know I'm not your mother," said Mrs. Garrett, "but you do be sure to be a gentleman at all times, and I know you will be." She paused and patted him on the arm. "Pour her hot chocolate first and give her the porcelain cup with the flowers on it. You can have the plain white one."

"Yes, ma'am."

"And I have a quilt and some hand warmers. Miss Beauchamp will be impressed that you thought of everything."

Doc chuckled. "Or rather that you thought of everything, dear."

Mrs. Garrett waved him away. "Now, now, Doc. You know what it's like to be young and in love."

And Solomon wished he knew what it was like to disappear. The heat flooded his face, and from the mischievous expression on Mrs. Garrett's face, he figured she noticed his embarrassment.

Doc placed a kiss on his wife's plump cheek. "Now, dear, we best hitch up the horses. I'm fairly sure the reverend here knows how to be gentlemanly and knows to give the object of his affection the pretty cup."

The object of his affection? Solomon stared at a thin crack in the floor. Yes, he had feelings for her. Strong feelings for her. But was it so obvious?

Mrs. Garrett's eyes widened and she waved Doc's comment aside. "Well, it never hurts to offer a reminder from time to time."

"Come along, Solomon. Sunlight is wasting. It'll be tomorrow before we send you on your way."

Solomon followed Doc to the barn where they hitched up the horses.

"I'm right proud of this here mode of transportation," Doc said. "It's a piano box sleigh manufactured back East. It has served me well all these years." He ran a hand over the faded green seat. "The upholstered seat is made of mohair."

Solomon didn't figure Doc and his wife to be older than forty, yet they both spoke as though they were much more advanced in years. "I'll take good care of the sleigh, sir."

"I know you will. I best find the crate the missus was asking for. If you wait long enough, she'll have an entire meal packed for you." He chuckled and placed his hands on his ample stomach. "I think it's time I took her on a sleigh ride again. We used to go quite often."

"She'd probably appreciate that, sir." But what did Solomon know about wives? He'd be fortunate just to survive courtship, let alone if he decided to marry someday. Lydie's beautiful face flashed through his mind. Would she agree to court him when he asked her today? He'd slept little last night thinking about how to ask her and what he'd do if she said "no."

Several minutes later, he and Doc returned to the house with the crate. Mrs. Garrett placed the pitcher, two cups, and two slices of bread inside, carefully packing everything so it wouldn't fall over in the sleigh. "The hot chocolate is a family recipe. There's sugar, cream, and a cinnamon stick in each. You tell that sweet young lady 'hello' for me."

"Will do. Thank you, ma'am." Solomon took the crate, along with the quilt and handwarmers and loaded them carefully into the sleigh. He bid the Garretts goodbye, promising once again to return the sleigh in an hour, then drove toward the Castleberry residence.

Ten times he nearly changed his mind and turned around to return the sleigh. Fifteen times he prayed for God's guidance and favor.

Lydie peered at the clock on the mantle above the Castleberry's fireplace. She wrapped her scarf around her neck and pulled on the black wool mittens the aunts had sent her. Solomon mentioned he had a surprise for her and would retrieve her at half past noon.

He was nearly fifteen minutes late.

Had he changed his mind?

Lydie paced the floor while ever so often gazing out the window to see if Solomon had arrived. Two weeks ago, she'd begun to have feelings for him, but wasn't sure he felt the same.

Mr. Castleberry was in town on an errand and Mrs. Castleberry was in her room reclining, so the house was quiet, except for the quiet whoosh of Mrs. Castleberry's muffled snores. Not that Lydie minded. As a more reserved person, she enjoyed her own company. And although she'd spent time with Solomon on other occasions, the fact that he had planned a surprise for her brought upon all sorts of feelings from anticipation and enthusiasm to curiosity and the jitters.

They'd met numerous times in the parlor after school. She'd learned so much about Solomon. His hopes, his dreams, and his past with a despicable grandfather. Yet, although she now spent a considerable amount of time with him, she couldn't wait to see him again.

Finally she heard a knock at the door. She opened it to find Solomon standing on the doorstep, a broad grin on his face.

A dimple shone in his chin and his hazel eyes crinkled at the corners. My but he was a handsome sort!

Heat whooshed up her face and neck. She most assuredly was staring.

"Hello, Lydie," he said, shoving his hands into his coat pockets.

"Hello, Solomon."

They stood for a few awkward moments before she remembered she had a voice. It helped that she had just noticed a sleigh parked not far from the front of the Castleberry's house. "Oh! Is that a sleigh?"

"It is. Shall we go for a ride?" He offered the crook of his elbow and she hooked her arm through it. "It's Doc's but he allowed us to borrow it for an hour."

"Oh, Solomon, this is delightful!"

He offered his hand to assist her into the sleigh. A pleasing tingle traveled up her arm when he remained holding her hand a few seconds longer than necessary. Solomon smiled at her. Should her heart be racing this fast?

Solomon released her hand and placed a quilt over her. "Courtesy of Mrs. Garrett," he said, the warmth of his smile echoed in his voice.

Lydie pressed the yellow and blue patchwork quilt against her legs. "That was thoughtful of her."

"Yes, and that's not all. She also provided handwarmers and some hot chocolate."

"Seems she thought of everything."

Solomon chuckled and climbed into the sleigh. He beckoned the horses and they began their smooth trek across the glistening snow.

A few robins, braving the brisk Wyoming Territory weather, chirped from their places in the pines. Solomon steered the sleigh with ease. Lydie closed her eyes for a moment and allowed the sun to shine on her face. When she'd spoken of wishing to someday take a sleigh ride, she hadn't known Solomon would make certain one of her fondest wishes would come true.

"I found this pond not far from town. It's frozen over now, but it's a sight to see with all the trees surrounding it."

"I would love to see that, Solomon."

He tossed her a grin and her heart raced all over again.

The ride outside of town was dotted with a few ranches and cabins tucked in groves of trees. In the distance, the mountains rose high above, their majesty giving testimony to an artistic Creator.

Solomon passed one final cabin, then stopped the sleigh in front of a pond surrounded by trees, their frozen and bare branches spindly spires of white providing a breathtaking view. He removed a timepiece from his coat pocket and checked the time. He ran a finger along the smooth gold plating before replacing it into this pocket. "It was my pa's." Solomon's distant gaze indicated he had been transported to a time long before the present. Lydie wanted to tell him she understood fully the yearnings of wishing your parents were still alive.

But she knew that, while they were both orphans, her circumstances were vastly different than his. Both orphans, yes, but she was well-cared by the aunts from the tender age of three when she'd lost her parents. Solomon's grandfather had not provided the compassionate, considerate, and benevolent care a young boy needed when he lost his parents.

"I almost forgot," Solomon said, reaching a hand toward the small crate on the floorboard by their feet. "Would you care for some hot chocolate? Mrs. Garrett says she made it with a special family recipe."

"She's a dear, and yes, I would love some hot chocolate." Homesickness at the thought of Aunt Fern's delicious hot chocolate with a peppermint stick flooded her mind and Lydie attempted to cast it aside. She'd not let anything ruin this time with Solomon.

He cautiously poured the hot chocolate into an ornate flowered cup and handed it to her, then proceeded to pour his own. The beverage had cooled a bit from being in the cold weather, but Lydie reveled in its cinnamon-laced flavor.

"Delicious," she said. Almost as delicious as Aunt Fern's, but she'd never divulge that to her aunt. She peered out over the frozen pond and a thought occurred to her. "Solomon, have you ever been ice skating?"

"No, can't say as I have."

"I'm surprised since you lived in Minnesota for a time."

Solomon gripped the mug in his hands, a distant expression crossing his face. "I never had the chance as a young'un. Not sure if we never thought of it or if there wasn't a pond nearby. There was one on the land near Grandfather's house, but..." his voice trailed.

Lydie placed a hand on his arm. "You needn't speak of it if you don't wish to."

"No, Lydie, it's...Grandfather wasn't keen on taking time from a workday to do frivolous things like ice skating. Nor allowing me to do so."

"I'm sorry."

"To him I was a workhorse who never did the work correctly." His tone turned somber, and at barely above a whisper, Lydie thought she may have misheard him. How devastating to a young boy to be thought of in such a manner. She knew he wrestled with the things of his past, and she longed to help him with a better future.

"Would you be willing to attempt ice skating?"

Solomon's easygoing demeanor returned. "I don't think that would be a wise idea. Seeing myself sprawled on the ice, one leg going this way and the other that way. Not a pleasing sight, especially for someone tall."

"What if I helped you? And before you say that would be an awkward circumstance seeing as how I couldn't very well catch you if you fell, let me just say I think you'd do better than you're anticipating."

"That thought did cross my mind." He paused, his handsomely rugged features causing her pulse to increase once again. "But if you're willing to give a lesson, I'm willing to try."

"Then let's make a plan. Perhaps we can find someone who has skates we could borrow."

Solomon flexed his right foot slightly as he examined it. "These are some big feet. Reckon we can find someone who has skates large enough?"

"I think we can."

They sat again in comfortable silence before Solomon beckoned the horses a short distance toward a dilapidated cabin. "I'm going to live here someday, Lydie."

The railing on the porch had fallen and an old wagon wheel, splintered and half-covered with a thick layer of snow, rested against the side of the house. There was a hole in the window and the roof sloped. She'd not say a word about the deteriorating condition. Not when Solomon's face shone of enthusiasm.

"I've been inside. It has potential. There are some broken stairs and some are just missing, but there's an upstairs and there's a rock fireplace and even an old table that I could refinish just as good as new." His eyes lit with excitement. "And as for this porch, can you see sitting on it in the evenings after a full day and relaxing in the shadow of those mountains?" He gestured toward the snow-capped mountains in the distance. "There's even an outhouse out back that needs only minor repairs. If I built a barn and got some chickens and a few head of cattle, it would supplement my earnings as a reverend." His words accelerated. "I've spoken with Mr. Castleberry at the bank and I could buy it at a reasonable price. Sure, I'd have to take a note out on it that would require me to pay on it for a lengthy time, but...it's doable, Lydie. Of that, I am sure. What do you think?"

That her opinion mattered to him so greatly touched her. She'd not say that she would merely pass such an eyesore by were she looking for a home. She'd not say that a lot of work would need to be done just to make it livable or that new lumber was pricey from what Mr. Morton said. No, she would share in his dream. "Yes, Solomon, I do believe it has potential."

He turned toward her so rapidly that the sleigh shook. A sense of urgency lined his tone. "Yes, and it would only take some elbow grease and I could trade work for some lumber, and I know how to build and repair things."

The hopeful look in his eyes was almost her undoing. "Yes, you do."

"And then it would be perfect for us." The second he said it, she noticed a bright red crept up his face. He turned rapidly from her and fidgeted with the button on his coat. "I mean..."

A ribbon of elation twirled within her. He was planning a future with her? This *could—would—*be their home? He would dedicate his time and effort into making it a suitable place to live? With her? Had Lydie heard correctly? Had he said "perfect for *us*?" Or was she merely being hopeful that he shared the same feelings she did?

Solomon slowly turned toward her. "I meant...it would be a nice place someday for..." his voice wavered and he cleared his throat. "I guess what I'm trying to say is...if I could say it without sounding like a cad. Uh..."

"Yes, Solomon."

"Yes, what?"

Would he ask her to court him? If so, her answer would certainly be "yes." Oh, the aunts would have to give their blessing, but she imagined they would without reservation. "Yes, Solomon Eliason, I will court you, if...if that's what you're asking."

"Yes, Lydie Beauchamp, that's exactly what I'm asking. And you will?"

"Yes, I will. Now, mind you, the aunts will have their say, but..."

His demeanor deflated slightly. "Are they still sore with me over the pranks?"

Lydie laughed. "Goodness no. They've forgiven you."

A whoosh of breath escaped his lips. "So you'll court me, then?"

"Yes."

They faced each other, in what Lydie determined to be awkward anticipation. Would he kiss her? She surely wanted him to. A fillip of excitement in her middle was enhanced when he leaned toward her. Lydie closed her eyes, wanting to remember this moment.

"May I steal a kiss from you, Lydie Beauchamp?"

Without opening her eyes, she answered, "Yes, Solomon Eliason, you may."

His lips gently claimed hers as he cupped her face. Her legs weakened and she was grateful she was sitting, rather than standing for she surely would have lost the ability to remain upright. The fluttery sensation in her stomach increased as the kiss continued. He smelled of pine and leather and his thumb tenderly stroked her cheek.

When they drew apart, their eyes met and she thought for a moment that he was going to kiss her again. Solomon brushed a gentle kiss across her forehead.

"We best head back so I can return Doc's sleigh," Solomon said.

Had all of this really happened? Had Solomon really asked to court her? And had he really kissed her? Lydie reached one hand toward her opposite arm and pinched herself.

Surely this wasn't a dream.

Chapter Twenty-Three

SOLOMON FINISHED WRITING DOWN the words for his next sermon when he heard a knock on the door.

"Abe, what brings you out today?"

"Be obliged if I could have a minute of your time."

Solomon ushered him inside. "Please, have a seat."

Abe planted himself on the only other chair in the house, a rickety wood one at the table. "Been needing to talk to you."

"Is everything all right?" Solomon sat in the chair at his desk.

"As you know, my daughter in Cheyenne has been after me to move there. I'm fixin' to do just that come spring when the weather clears. Someone has expressed interest in purchasing the ranch and some of the cattle. I'm not keen on driving the rest of them to Cheyenne. It's gonna take forever to travel there myself, let alone with a herd of cows."

Solomon would miss Abe. He understood his friend's hankering to be near his daughter, but Solomon had come to see him as a mentor and grandfather of sorts. "I would be remiss if I didn't say I'd miss you."

"I know, son, and I'll miss you too. Now here's what I'm thinking...I have about twenty head of cattle and a bunch of chickens and one rooster. How about they find a new home out at the old

Foss place? I hear from Castleberry that you're fixin' to purchase it."

"Yes, sir, I am. But it would take me some time to pay you back."

"Not looking for you to pay me back. It would be a gift."

Solomon attempted to utter the words thanking Abe, but instead his vocal cords refused to work.

"Come spring," Abe continued, "I'll help you get them to that new place of yours. We'll build a corral. Already talked to Townsend, Morton, Doc, and Castleberry. They're ready to build a barn. Guy named Campbell said he knew you and he wanted to help too."

"I don't...I don't know what to say." Emotion welled in Solomon's throat. They would do this for him? Abe would *give* him cattle and chickens? The elders and Castleberry offered to help build the barn? Campbell would join them? "I...thank you."

Abe stood. "You're welcome. I consider you a grandson, Solomon. I've got a passel full of granddaughters, but you're my only grandson."

"Sir..."

"Sir is a sign of respect, and I appreciate you calling me that. But if you'd like, you may call me Grandpa Abe. I know I'll be in Cheyenne, but I aim to make the weeklong ride to visit Willow Falls now and then and I'll write."

The words remained wedged in his throat. "I...thank you, Abe, Grandpa Abe."

"Sure thing. I'm honored to have you as a grandson and thankful you'll give my animals a new home. Now I best get. I heard from Mrs. Morton that you're joining a certain young lady for ice skating." Abe winked. "I always knew you fancied her, what with the way you talked about her and all."

Had he been that obvious? "She thinks she can teach me how to ice skate."

"Well, with the skates the Mortons are lending you and her being a teacher, I don't see why a man such as yourself can't learn. Just don't fall." Abe chuckled and squeezed Solomon's shoulder.

"Thank you again. For everything, Grandpa Abe."

As Solomon watched the man leave, three things resonated with him. One, he now had a grandfather who cared about him. Second, he could never repay Abe's kindness and what it meant to be adopted by a man who wasn't even related by blood. And third, he prayed someday God would allow him to show the same kindness to someone else.

The Mortons skated to the far end of the pond while Lydie and Solomon put on the borrowed skates. "I'm not sure about this," Solomon muttered.

"You'll do fine. It'll just take some practice."

He pointed at the Mortons. Mr. Morton twirled Mrs. Morton perfectly on the ice. "But they make it look so easy." Would he someday be able to twirl Lydie on the ice? Or would today be the first *and* last day of his ice skating adventure?

"They've likely been practicing for a long time." Lydie offered her hand to assist him from the rock on which he sat. The last thing he wanted was to cause Lydie to fall so he took her hand, but managed to push himself from the rock into a standing position.

He teetered on the blades and had an urgent desire to flee, but not on the skates.

"Walk carefully to the pond," Lydie instructed. She tucked her arm through his.

Solomon wobbled, attempting to keep his balance. If it was this challenging in the snow, what would it be like on slippery ice?

They reached the pond and Lydie stood facing him. She extended both hands to him. "I'll go backwards and you go forward."

Solomon never minded being six feet, two inches before today. "It's a long way down."

Lydie giggled, her sweet tinkling laugh calming his anxiety somewhat.

"Now, one foot then the other. Just glide."

It was his turn to laugh. "Glide? I'll be fortunate if I can manage to stay upright."

They scooted their way gingerly along the ice until his feet slipped from beneath him. He let go of Lydie's hands, flailed his arms, and fell hard to the ice below.

"Solomon?" Lydie's frantic tone rang in his ears as he attempted to salvage his pride.

"I'm fine, Lydie."

She leaned over and faced him. "Are you sure?"

The compassion in her eyes reminded him yet again why he was falling in love with her. He leaned toward her and brushed his lips against hers. He'd endure ice skating every day of his life if it meant time with Lydie.

Eight falls later—yes, he'd counted—and Solomon had an infinitesimal grasp on what it meant to remain in a standing position while on two uncomfortable ice skates.

Chapter Twenty-Four

IT WAS CHRISTMAS EVE, and tomorrow Solomon planned to ask Lydie to marry him. The thought occurred to him that he would need the approval from two important individuals.

Solomon re-read the letter. Would Lydie's aunts agree to his proposal?

Dear Aunt Myrtle and Aunt Fern,
I would have liked to ask you this in person, but a letter will have to suffice.

He paused. Did he sound intelligent and forthright? Smart but not stuffy? He wanted the aunts to think highly of him and not that he was some uneducated oaf. Book learning had always come easily to him, as had writing, vocabulary, and recitation. Thankfully he would not have to do arithmetic to win their favor.

I have fallen in love with your niece. As such, I am hereby requesting your blessing to marry her. She is kind, thoughtful, cares deeply for the downtrodden, and is a good teacher. She's beautiful and possesses a nice sense of humor. I would like nothing more than to make her my wife.

Lydie has mentioned many times your devout care for her since she was a child. I promise you I'll do my best to give her the life she deserves, a loving husband, a roof over her head, and food.

Solomon stared at the last sentence. He hoped he could be a loving husband. His mind reverted to the cabin. The roof was in poor shape, but he intended to fix that before they set a wedding date. *If* Lydie accepted. He peered at the shelf in the parsonage. The variety and quantity of foodstuffs was dismal: two cans of beans in tomato sauce, a bag of flour, a half a loaf of bread, and two jars of jam. Sure, he ate at the homes of others most nights, but if he aimed to provide for a wife, he would need more food than the meager offerings on the shelf.

He thought of the cabin once again. Was it suitable for a wife? The image of rodents running through it crossed his mind. He had seen evidence while there the most recent time he visited. Would he be able to afford a new window to replace the broken one? Would someone as respectable as Lydie find the cabin sufficient enough?

What if Lydie said "no" to his Christmas proposal? What if she didn't feel for him the way he felt for her? Fears and uncertainties niggled their way into his mind. Would he be a good husband? Would he someday be a good father like his own pa? Or would he be harsh and unloving like Grandfather? What if he couldn't make enough money to support them? What if he couldn't keep his word to Mr. Castleberry and he defaulted on the bank note?

Perhaps he ought to wait until next spring to propose to her.

Another thought occurred to him: if she did decline to marry him, what would the aunts think of his letter? His struggle to write it coherently would be for naught. He feared he was being presumptuous in asking for their blessing before he'd even asked for Lydie's hand.

Solomon reached for his Bible and flipped through the pages to First Peter. He'd spent considerable time underlining more verses yesterday during his time with the Lord. *"Casting all your care upon him; for he careth for you."*

He bowed his head and gave his concerns to the Lord. Was it His will that Solomon make Lydie his wife?

He continued reading his letter to Lydie's aunts.

I promise I will be worthy of her, love her as Christ loved the church, and provide for her.

Thank you for your consideration.

Sincerely,

Solomon Eliason

He folded the letter, placed it in an envelope, addressed it to Myrtle and Fern Beauchamp, Prune Creek, Wyoming Territory, then walked to the post office to mail it.

A church service commenced in the afternoon, followed by the festivities as Morton's Mercantile. The back room was the only place in town large enough to host a sizeable group and there was plenty of room for tables with goodies.

Fifteen minutes before the event started, townsfolk crowded into the mercantile and the students of the Willow Falls school took their places at the front.

"What if I don't remember the songs?" Richard asked.

Frederick placed a comforting hand on his shoulder. "You will. You've sung them for years."

"All right, students," said Solomon. "Are you ready?"

Eleven heads nodded. Solomon gazed out at the throng of people. His eyes connected with Lydie's and he almost forgot to proceed. While the Christmas surprise of the choir didn't replace time with her aunts, he hoped it helped alleviate some of her discouragement at being away from them at Christmas.

"Thank you for coming to hear our Christmas choir. We have four songs to sing to you this evening and then we'll enjoy some of Mrs. Townsend's gingerbread cookies."

Tears brimmed in Lydie's eyes. She'd told Solomon how delightful it would be to have a Christmas choir, and he'd worked diligently to bring her dream to fruition. Just as he had the sleigh ride. His words as they walked to the mercantile earlier in the evening sounded in her ears. *"I want this to be a special holiday for you, Lydie. I know this is your first Christmas without your aunts."*

Tomorrow evening, they would attend Christmas dinner at the Castleberry home.

If she couldn't be with Aunt Myrtle and Aunt Fern, spending time with Solomon and receiving his kind thoughtfulness made the loneliness subside.

The students began with *Good King Wenceslas*, and Solomon waved a ruler, using it as a conductor's baton. It was obvious the pupils had vehemently practiced. When they finished the song, the townsfolk clapped and the children then sang *O Come, All Ye Faithful; Good Christian Men, Rejoice;* and concluded with *Silent Night.*

One thing Lydie noticed immediately was that, unlike the first day of school, they were all in synchronized harmony. How long had Solomon practiced with them and how had she not known of this surprise until tonight?

She placed a hand to her bosom as joyful tears emerged. She'd found a good man in Solomon Eliason.

When the students finished, Doc Garrett strolled to the front of the room. He praised the children, then added, "Before we partake in gingerbread cookies, we have a special announcement." Mrs. Garrett handed him a thick, wrapped parcel. "This gift is presented to a newcomer to our community. Someone who selflessly gives to others. As most of you are likely unaware, this individual used his own funds to purchase hymnals for the congregation."

Several murmurs echoed in the room.

"Please join me in thanking Reverend Solomon."

Solomon stepped forward, a red hue staining his face. Doc handed him the parcel. "Thank you, son, for all you do for our town."

"Open it! Open it!" exclaimed Richard.

Solomon removed the paper and gasped. "Thank you," he said, holding up the new brown coat.

"Try it on," one of the students suggested.

Solomon did as was requested. The wool coat fit perfectly and accentuated his broad shoulders.

Lydie hadn't known he'd funded the hymnals with his own money. His generosity was just another reason she was drawn to him.

Frederick peered around Doc Garrett. "I saw that coat first when it arrived at the mercantile. I even tried it on. Didn't fit real good." The boy's antics always brought a smile to Lydie's face.

Mrs. Castleberry bustled to the front of the room. "May I say something, Doc?" she asked.

Doc waved a hand at her. "Please do."

She pressed her hands on the skirt of her elaborate pale green dress. "When my husband and I first moved here, I didn't realize how much I would miss playing the piano. I was trained by a distinguished pianist back East and became an accomplished and proficient pianist in my own right." She firmed her posture. "When entertaining Reverend Solomon in our home in recent days as he visited Miss Beauchamp, I've come to realize how much I miss playing the piano on a consistent basis. After much discussion with my husband, we have agreed to temporarily move the instrument to the church. When the new piano arrives from Denver in the coming months, we will donate that one and return my piano to our home."

Mrs. Castleberry turned toward Solomon. "Reverend, with your blessing, I would delight in being allowed to play the hymns for Sunday service."

For the second time that night, Solomon's expression turned to one of surprise. His mouth fell open, and once again, red flushed his face. "We would be honored to have you play the piano for church."

"Fabulous! This is such a blithesome moment and I assure you, you'll not be disappointed."

Later that evening, Solomon accompanied Lydie to the Castleberry home. The air had grown colder with a hint of more snow.

Solomon wore his new coat, a significant improvement over his former tattered one. "Did you know about the coat?" he asked.

"I did, although it wasn't my idea." She thought of how Mrs. Morton had mentioned it to her at the mercantile. Mrs. Garrett thought of it after seeing Solomon in his threadbare coat the day he arrived to borrow the sleigh.

"I honestly can't believe the town would do something like this. I'm humbled."

"I can believe it," Lydie said. "People have grown fond of you over the past several weeks." *I've grown fond of you.*

Solomon slowed their pace as they came to a patch of ice. He held onto her a little tighter as they traversed the treacherous area. "It wasn't long ago I thought I should move on from Willow Falls."

"Sometimes folks take a while to adjust to a newcomer. But they now see you for the godly man you are." She paused. "Thank you again for making Christmas special."

She peered up at his handsome profile. He faced her, and although she couldn't see much in the dark night, she had a hunch his hazel eyes twinkled. "You're welcome."

They arrived at the Castleberry home a minutes later. Solomon stepped inside to bid her goodbye. "I'll see you tomorrow for Christmas supper." He stroked her cheek with his thumb. "Good night, Lydie."

She felt warmth flow through her. Tomorrow couldn't come soon enough.

CHAPTER TWENTY-FIVE

CHRISTMAS AT THE CASTLEBERRY home proved to be memorable. After supper, Lydie, Solomon, and Mr. Castleberry gathered around the piano while Mrs. Castleberry played Christmas tunes on the piano.

They began with *Hark! The Herald Angels Sing* followed by *Joy to the World, O Come, All Ye Faithful,* and *Silent Night.* Lydie stood next to Solomon, and twice his fingers brushed against her hand. Her stomach fluttered and she attempted to return her attention to singing.

His rich baritone voice as he sang caused her to pause her own caroling for a moment to listen.

"Well, I could certainly play well into the night," said Mrs. Castleberry, after a melodic rendition of *Silent Night.* "But alas, presents and supper are calling us."

"Yes, dear, and you could play well into the night and then some," teased Mr. Castleberry. "We almost didn't make it to church yesterday and the festivities afterwards because she nearly remained planted on her piano bench."

Mrs. Castleberry held her chin high. "Yes, and just a warning, Reverend Solomon, hymns might constitute a fair portion of our Sunday services."

They joined in laughter before taking their places on the chairs and settee once again in anticipation for Christmas gifts. When it came time for Lydie to present Solomon with his gift, she retreated to the kitchen. High on the shelf and hidden beneath a tea towel was the apple pie.

She hoped he liked it.

"I believe you'll need to close your eyes," suggested Mrs. Castleberry.

Lydie walked carefully into the parlor, watching her step as she carried the pie. The aroma of apples waffled in the air. She placed the pie in Solomon's outstretched hands.

"You may open your eyes," said Mrs. Castleberry, being quite the helpful sort.

"Lydie, this looks delicious!" Solomon rose. "Would it be bad etiquette, Mrs. Castleberry, if I cut a slice right now?"

Mrs. Castleberry shook her head and gestured toward the table. "Not at all."

Mr. Castleberry followed Solomon. "Mind if I have a..." he turned to face Mrs. Castleberry. "A sliver?"

"A sliver indeed," chortled Mrs. Castleberry.

"I was once a skinny gent. While we've had hired help for many years now, it was my beloved wife's fine culinary talents that caused me to become, ahem, slightly rotund." He winked at his wife.

Mrs. Castleberry blushed. "All right, have a slice rather than a sliver."

Solomon cut the pie and placed a piece on his plate. Lydie held her breath as he took a bite. She needn't have worried.

"This is delicious, Lydie. It's hard to believe you and Aunt Myrtle are related."

A giggle rose in Lydie's throat. "Oh, yes, our dear Aunt Myrtle has many admirable talents. Cooking and baking are not among them."

"I heard about that atrocious huckleberry pie at the potluck. Your aunt seemed like a delightful woman, but I'm thankful Mrs. Morton's huckleberries didn't go to waste," said Mrs. Castleberry.

"Indeed," chuckled Mr. Castleberry. "Frederick is one of the few people who savors burnt crusts and salty fruit."

"I have a gift for you now," said Solomon, after he'd finished his second slice. He returned to the Christmas tree and retrieved a tiny parcel.

Lydie removed the wrap to find a tin of sugar plum candies. "The aunts treated me to a tin of these when we lived in Minnesota."

An easy smile played at the corners of Solomon's mouth. "I, too, have tried them. And it was no easy feat finding a tin that hadn't been sampled by Frederick."

After presents and supper, Mr. and Mrs. Castleberry retreated to the parlor, leaving Lydie and Solomon alone at the table. He took her hands in his. A jolt of tingles zipped up her arm and her heart raced.

"Lydie..."

His expression had become so serious. Was everything all right? Had the food not agreed with him? Was he still contemplating leaving Willow Falls? Her heart sank. Lydie was about to ask when he continued.

"I...uh..."

"Yes, Solomon? What is it?"

As if he hadn't heard her, he resumed. "Oh, I know I'll need the blessing of your aunts, and I've already thought of that." He stroked her hand tenderly with his thumb and she thought she might not hear another word he said for her heart beat so loudly in her ears. Was he about to propose?

"You see, I already wrote a letter asking for their blessing. I know we've only courted a short time and I'm willing to court you as long as necessary. Lydie, will you marry me?"

Relief flooded over her and she uttered the words without hesitation. "Yes!"

"I left Minnesota with only the clothes I was wearing. But I do own a fine horse, a Bible, a few foodstuffs on the shelf in the parsonage, and a new winter coat. And come spring, I'll be the owner of the Foss place. Yes, I know the roof slopes, but I aim to make it as good as new. I'll replace the window and repair the broken stairs. Abe taught me a lot about carpentry in the past few months, and several of the menfolk will be assisting me in building a barn. Abe promised me several head of cattle and some chickens to get us started. I'm a hard worker and will be doing other jobs besides preaching if need be to support us."

"Yes, Solomon."

Mrs. Castleberry peered around the corner, a hint of merriment in her eyes, before presumably returning to her chair in the parlor to read her new book.

"I know, Lydie, I know you knew most of this already, but I just wanted to reiterate that while I don't have much right now, I *can* and *will* provide for you. I promise you'll never go hungry or be without a home." He paused as if to catch his breath after the rapid streaming of his words. "I love you, Lydie Beauchamp, and I promise on my honor to be worthy of you and not allow anyone to play pranks on you again."

"Solomon..."

"I know, I'm a verbose man at times. I just want to reassure you that while I may not have much by way of possessions and I'll likely never be wealthy, I will see to it that you are loved and cherished."

"I will marry you."

"And I figure we can serve others together like when we took the meal to Mr. and Mrs. Hurley."

"I will marry you," she repeated, a little louder this time.

His jaw went slack and he stared as if her words had yet to resonate. "Did you say you'll marry me?"

Lydie giggled. "Yes, Solomon Eliason, I will marry you."

In a rapid movement, Solomon stood, assisted her to her feet, and swung her weightless into his strong arms.

"Is everything all right in here?" Mr. Castleberry wandered in from the parlor and grabbed another gingerbread cookie.

Solomon set her on her feet again. "Oh, yes, sir. It's more than all right. Lydie just agreed to be my wife."

Mr. Castleberry smirked. "Congratulations." He waved a hand. "Carry on, then."

⸙

Lydie couldn't sleep that night. Solomon's declaration of love for her and his marriage proposal still lingered in her mind. A quick kiss at the doorway before he left for home confirmed the reality of all that had transpired.

She swung her legs over the side of the bed, lit the lamp, and began to pen a letter to the aunts.

Dearest Aunt Myrtle and Aunt Fern,
I can't wait to share some exciting news with you...

Epilogue

THE WEATHER WAS PERFECT for a wedding and after the vows, everyone offered well-wishes as Solomon and Lydie walked down the church steps and toward the waiting wagon.

"I always knew Solomon was a fine young man," quipped Aunt Fern.

"And you knew that how?" challenged Aunt Myrtle.

Aunt Fern rolled her eyes. "That's easy. I knew he was a fine young man because he bravely ate your huckleberry pie. And I knew he had a strong constitution because he didn't die from it."

"Oh, pshaw!"

"You didn't realize you were inheriting two aunts when you said your wedding vows," giggled Lydie.

Solomon didn't mind. He would have inherited five hundred crazy aunts just to win Lydie's heart.

As they rode out of town toward their new home, the one that now boasted a fixed roof and window, clean floors, and some furniture, he thought of their future.

Much had changed over the course of the past few months.

The church slowly grew and Mr. and Mrs. Symons had begun attending.

The new piano arrived and Mrs. Castleberry took her role as the church pianist very seriously.

Frederick was given a ride in the stagecoach to prepare him to someday drive one.

Solomon finally was able to preach his sermon on forgiveness, and with God's help, he was able to forgive Grandfather for the pain he'd caused.

Solomon pulled the wagon to the side of the road and took his wife in his arms.

"I love you, Mrs. Eliason," he said.

"And I love you, Mr. Eliason."

He then sealed the vows he'd made with a kiss.

Author's Note

Love's New Beginnings was a pleasant surprise. After readers asked me to write a story about Lydie and Solomon, I set out to do just that. I had no idea where the characters and story would lead or if it would ever be published. I'm thrilled the book did come to fruition, and it was especially exciting to discover it would be a Christmas release (my first one in the over-a-dozen books I've written).

Love's New Beginnings gave me a chance to show Solomon's background and how he grew into a wise and beloved mentor. Of course, Lydie is a sweetheart and was later able to give motherly counsel to Annie in *Forgotten Memories* and Hannah in *Dreams of the Heart*. Writing this book also gave me a good starting point to introduce Aunt Myrtle and Aunt Fern. If you would like to see the visual inspiration for my characters and the setting, please visit my Pinterest page.

The Wyoming Territory was a rough and rowdy place in the mid-1800s. Indian wars were common and the Wyoming Territory was known for some famous Indian battles including those at Fort Phil Kearney, the Wind River, and at Three Crossings. Wyoming is also known for famous outlaws such as Butch Cassidy and Harry Longabaugh, aka the Sundance Kid. For purposes of the story, I didn't focus on these items.

Fictional liberties were taken, including founding towns sooner than they were likely settled in Wyoming, especially in the northern part of the state, which is the setting for the Wyoming Sunrise series.

According to my research, there really were, at times, caskets in the mercantiles. And stagecoach etiquette was a real thing. Also during my research, I discovered a plethora of items people ate in the 1800s ate. Did you know that people ate skunks back in the olden days? Not a regular delicacy, but they did eat them on occasion. After reading about the ingredients for mock turtle soup and discovering about skunks for dinner (aka supper), I'm even more grateful for enchiladas and regular plain ol' hamburgers.

Who will we see more of in future books? In *Forgotten Memories*, Lydie and Solomon have a family of their own. We'll briefly visit again with Sheriff Townsend, Doc, and Mr. and Mrs. Morton.

I have it on good authority that the aunts will play prominent roles in Charlotte's story, *When Love Comes*. And Frederick will reappear in *Dreams of the Heart*. I've already had feedback from readers saying they'd like to see a novella about Frederick as a man, and of course keeping him just as ornery.

ACKNOWLEDGMENTS

To my family. I can never thank you enough for your encouragement, support, and patience as I put words to paper. I'm so grateful for you. Thank you for your patient endurance in living with an author who spends her time predominately in the 1800s (and sometimes forgets to come back to the present).

To my oldest daughter, who is a fellow author and a knowledgeable historian. Thank you for brainstorming with me and for all of your historical insight.

To my Penny's Peeps Street Team. Thank you for spreading the word about my books. I appreciate your support!

To my readers. May God bless and guide you as you grow in your walk with Him.

And, most importantly, thank you to my Lord and Savior, Jesus Christ. It is my deepest desire to glorify You with my writing and help bring others to a knowledge of Your saving grace.

If you enjoyed this glimpse into the lives of Lydie and Solomon, please consider leaving a review on your social media and favorite retailer sites. Reviews are critical to authors, and those stars you give us are such an encouragement.

If you enjoyed *Love's New Beginnings*, you won't want to miss the next book in the series, *Forgotten Memories,* which is Annie and Caleb's story.

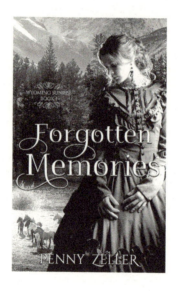

Keep reading for a peek inside *Forgotten Memories.*

WYOMING TERRITORY, 1877

A FLEETING MOVEMENT CAUGHT twelve-year-old Annie Ledbetter's attention. She squinted at the grove of trees on a distant hill and willed her eyes to focus. A quick flash of something—or someone—appeared. Annie tipped her head to the left and stood on tiptoe, anticipating a better view.

The vacant prairie previously held nothing but miles and miles of grasslands, sagebrush, and the occasional rolling hill.

Until now.

Annie's feet stalled in the soft dirt as if rooted. Could it be? A man, or maybe more than one man, watched and scrutinized Annie and the rest of the travelers.

But as quickly as the figure appeared, he vanished.

A shiver of fear traveled up her spine.

Annie's heart skipped a beat and her arms tingled with numbness. What had she just seen? She rubbed her eyes and took a second glance, but now saw nothing. Stumbling, she began to walk again.

Should she mention what she had seen to Pa? Surely Pa, with his perceptive eyesight, had noticed the elusive movement. In the wagon, he and Ma carried on what appeared to be an important conversation, although Annie couldn't hear the words over the creaking of the wagon wheels and the commotion from the other families in their wagon train. Ma nodded at whatever Pa said, her hands propped comfortably on her large belly. The baby would be here soon.

Hopefully they made it to Nelsonville before that happened.

Annie stared in the direction of the grove of trees. Had she imagined what she'd seen? After all, Ma had commented on more than one occasion that Annie had an overabundance of imagination. If so, best not to tell Pa. He and her brother, Zeb, would give her a good ribbing about how the lonely boredom on the journey from their home in Hollins, Nebraska, to the Wyoming Territory caused her to conjure up things that weren't really there. From the beginning of their trip several days ago, it had been an uneventful adventure with no Indian attacks, no severe illness among the travelers, and no unexpected deaths. Why should that change?

Annie rubbed her stomach then and groaned, attempting to appease the intermittent discomfort. Was it nervousness from what she thought she saw or were the berries she'd eaten at lunch causing a disturbance?

"Hiya, Annie." Zeb ran up alongside her and matched his steps with hers.

Annie diverted her attention from her nausea and turned to face her fourteen-year-old brother. She weighed her options. *Should I tell him about what I saw? Surely there would be no end to the teasing, but maybe he saw it too.*

"I think I saw someone hidden behind those trees."

Zeb shielded his eyes from the sun and focused where she pointed. "I don't see anyone."

"It must have been my imagination." Annie sighed and brushed aside a stray hair that had fallen from one of her braids.

Zeb's confirmation somehow soothed her, yet her stomach was still in upheaval. "I wonder if we'll stop soon for supper."

To rest for a while sounded appealing.

"Our noonday meal wasn't that long ago. Are you all right?"

"I think the wild berries are causing a fuss in my stomach."

"Perhaps you can ride in the wagon for a spell."

Without awaiting her response, Zeb garnered Pa's attention, and moments later, Annie climbed into the back of the wagon, anxious to lie down in the hopes of settling her stomach.

The canvas provided a respite from the sun, even if the space was hot, crowded, and stuffy. The wagon housed all they owned and didn't leave much room for a growing twelve-year-old girl. Listless, Annie reached for her diary, the simple, well-worn book that had long ago become her companion. Perhaps penning an entry would relieve her nerves. She opened it and began to write for the first time since leaving her home.

July 14, 1877

Dear Diary,

Pa says we will soon be reaching Nelsonville in the Wyoming Territory. I, for one, am thankful we are almost to our new home.

Having lost nearly everything and having to start over has been difficult for Ma and Pa, and I revisit often the memories of our old soddie and the mismatched round table and four chairs Grandpa Ledbetter gave Ma and Pa on their wedding day. I miss supper with stew, cornmeal muffins, and apple pie for dessert. Much more decadent than the plain beans we eat day after day on our journey.

Only one other family in our wagon train will settle in Nelsonville. Everyone else will continue to other destinations.

I had a nervous fright today when I thought I saw something in the distance, perhaps a man. I pray it was only my imagination.

Caleb Ryerson stood beside his horse and watched as his older brother, Cain, peered through a brass monocular spyglass. Another plot to commit a crime. Would Cain and his friend, Roy, ever tire of taking things that didn't belong to them? Would they ever tire of ruining the lives of others?

Cain snickered. "You won't believe this, but that ain't no stagecoach that's comin'. It's a band of wagons."

He was crouched out of sight behind a grove of trees overlooking the valley where the travelers journeyed.

"What? I thought we was supposed to be watching for a stagecoach. Give me that." Roy Fuller grabbed the spyglass from Cain and peered through it. "Well I'll be. Little wagon train, likely four or five wagons."

Roy spit to the side, barely missing Cain's foot.

"Don't matter none, though. We can rob them just the same as we rob a stagecoach. And anyways, we might even get more loot out of the deal." Roy lifted the spyglass and gazed through it again. "Definitely ain't no big wagon train."

"I think we should stick to stagecoaches," Caleb interjected.

"Keep your opinions to yourself, Little Brother, 'cause no one even asked you," snapped Cain. "I'm tired of you trying to make 'polite' decisions. This ain't no time for politeness. As I've told you a dozen times, if you wanna eat, you'll do as I say. It's as simple as that."

Caleb sighed and kicked the soft dirt with the toe of his worn boot. He, Cain, and Roy had taken to robbing stagecoaches in a variety of Wyoming and Dakota Territory towns. Oftentimes, the loot was bountiful and the thievery simple. Twice there had been casualties. He cringed at the thought of his brother's and Roy's disregard for life and willed the memories to vanish from his mind. Those casualties had been someone's pa, brother, or son. He had never participated in taking the life of another and never would. His conscience wouldn't let him. If he someday wanted to leave the lifestyle he'd been born into, Caleb knew he would have to abstain from as much crime as possible, even if it meant suffering Cain's wrath.

"It pays better than trying to earn a living the honest way," Cain told Caleb on more than one occasion. "We're so good ain't no one ever gonna catch us. You'd think they'd have better lawmen in this part of the country."

Maybe the lawmen were smart and luck played a major role in their failure to be apprehended. What would happen someday when there was no more luck? Prison time? Hangings? Death from a gunfight like what happened to Pa? Caleb shivered. Would he ever escape the life he lived?

The coarse conversation between Cain and Roy drew Caleb back to the present. He attempted to ignore their discussions until Cain directed a question at him. "What do you say, Caleb?"

Caleb cleared his throat. "I'm just saying these are probably families without much. Let's wait for the stagecoach."

Hearing himself attempt to dissuade Cain and Roy made his insides churn. Yes, while he was trying to talk them out of robbing a wagon train, he was consenting to rob yet another stagecoach. No matter who they robbed, stealing was stealing and Caleb knew, although no one had ever taught him so, that stealing was wrong.

"I don't care what you think or what you say," Cain sneered. "Look at your hand. Do you want to work for someone who does that to you again?"

Caleb rubbed a finger over the wide three-inch-long diagonal burn scar on his hand. No, he never wanted to work for someone like the mean Mr. Yager again. A man whose punishment included a hot piece of steel seared into Caleb's flesh as a permanent reminder of his wrongdoing.

Still, the thought of stealing from families unsettled him. There had to be a better way to make a living.

"Now, here's the plan. Caleb, you're gonna be the one to find the loot inside the wagons. You'll raid them and take anything you see worthy of selling. And I mean *anything*. Sometimes these folks have coins and jewelry, so be lookin' for that." Cain handed him a burlap sack. "Roy and me, we're gonna order everyone off the wagons before the search and we'll be sure no one fights back. There's likely to be at least one man in each wagon, so we don't want to be overpowered. 'Course, if anyone decides to give us any guff or attempts to reach for a gun, we'll shoot them."

Roy chuckled. "I like this plan. I always get the fun parts." He pulled his Colt .45 Peacemaker from its holster and ran his left forefinger over the barrel. "This gun has served me well."

Caleb had never shot anyone and never would unless it was in self-defense. He just wasn't like Cain and Roy. They'd killed before and hadn't thought much of it. They'd once been apprentices in a life of crime. Now they were professionals, shooting anyone who dared cross their path. Caleb recalled a time only a few months ago when Cain had threatened to take Caleb's life for disagreeing with something he and Roy said. It was that memory that reminded him not to provoke the two any further.

"Did you hear what I said, Little Brother?" Cain snapped, elbowing Caleb hard enough to nearly knock him off his feet.

"Yes." He struggled to maintain an upright position as pain shot through his side.

"Ain't no way and no how Caleb's ever gonna shoot nobody," sneered Roy. "You ain't never shot no one, have you, you stupid fool? Think you're better than me and Cain anyways, just 'cause you ain't never shot no one. Maybe we should just leave the coward here while we take care of business."

"It would be the easier way," Cain agreed. "But, if he wants to eat supper tonight, he's gonna have to help. I know I, for one, am not going to continue to support someone who doesn't work for their meals. There ain't no free supper to be had here."

Roy nodded. "So is you in or ain't you?" he asked Caleb.

"I'm in."

Caleb didn't want to let the thought of hunger cross his mind. He'd been hungry too many times in his life. In response to the thought of food and lack thereof, his stomach rumbled. If only he could make a decent living—maybe own a ranch or apprentice for a local merchant. Instead, his destiny had been planned for him—a destiny that included stealing what didn't belong to him. His father had been an outlaw. Now he and Cain followed in Alvin Ryerson's footsteps. Caleb couldn't deny the trapped feeling smothering him when he thought of the lack of choices he had for his future.

What about the innocent people whose lives would soon change at the hands of Cain and Roy? Had it been Caleb's choice, he would have asked the people in the wagon train if they would be willing to share their supper with him in exchange for work. Cain, of course, had different plans. He believed he was owed everything. Entitled. How could two brothers born of the same parents be so different? He reasoned with himself that Cain was a lot like what Caleb remembered of their father. He recalled the times their pa had taken them on what Alvin termed "jobs". Cain had gleaned what he could from watching Alvin Ryerson in action. Caleb had closed his eyes and begged to be taken home. Such a response received nothing less than a tongue lashing followed by a whipping from Pa. He still had the scars to prove it.

"They better have some loot, that's all I gotta say," Roy grumbled with a scowl. "I don't believe in wastin' no time."

"They probably don't have much," Caleb muttered.

"You don't know that, you stupid idiot." Cain again jabbed his elbow into his brother's ribs. "If they're moving, it's likely they have everything they own. Wouldn't you take some money with you if you were moving? 'Course, maybe not, since you ain't that smart."

"Yes, I would take money with me," Caleb answered. He took his hat off and wiped his brow with his forearm. How had he and Cain come to this? His brother was only seventeen and already a hardened criminal. Their father had been dead for six years and for those six years, they'd fought to survive. Caleb shuddered at how things transpired since they'd become orphans.

He never thought he'd be an outlaw at the age of fourteen.

Roy let loose a string of swear words. "Is you comin' or is you just gonna stand there and look dumb?"

Caleb wished he could be anywhere but here at this moment. As he always did when they planned a heist, he covered his face with the handkerchief so only his eyes were visible. He pulled his dingy cowboy hat low over his forehead as he'd been instructed and followed his brother and Roy toward the unsuspecting travelers.

Annie wasn't sure how long she'd been asleep in the back of the wagon, nestled against the rough edges of the trunks, when a loud noise startled her. She sat up and shook away the feeling of pins and needles in her right leg from holding it in one position too long.

She no longer heard her father's low rumble of laughter or her mother's sweet singing of their favorite hymns as they rode across the prairie. Those noises had been replaced by raucous, unknown male voices, a woman shrieking, and a young child crying.

Was she still asleep and having a dream?

Was her creative mind once again getting the best of her?

Annie fluttered her eyes, attempting to rid herself of the drowsiness that remained from her nap. Somewhere nearby a horse neighed.

More yelling.

More commotion.

"Ma?"

No answer.

Annie inched to where she could see out of the back of the wagon. It was then she saw something that horrified her—nothing made of imagination, but something of pure reality.

If only she had told Pa.

ABOUT THE AUTHOR

Penny Zeller is known for her heartfelt stories of faith and her passion to impact lives for Christ through fiction. While she has had a love for writing since childhood, she began her adult writing career penning articles for national and regional publications on a wide variety of topics. Today, Penny is the author of over a dozen books. She is also a homeschool mom and a fitness instructor.

When Penny is not dreaming up new characters, she enjoys spending time with her husband and two daughters, camping, hiking, canoeing, reading, running, cycling, gardening, and playing volleyball.

She is represented by Tamela Hancock Murray of the Steve Laube Agency and loves to hear from her readers at her website and her blog, *random thoughts from a day in the life of a wife, mom, and author.*

Social Media Links:
https://linktr.ee/pennyzeller

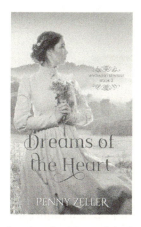

Sometimes the hardest battles take place in the heart.

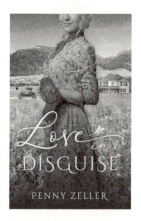

Who knew concealing one's true identity could be so disastrous?

He builds houses. She builds websites.
Together, can they build a family for two orphans?

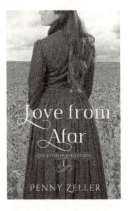

What happens when two little sisters become
self-appointed matchmakers?

Will a best friend's matchmaking scheme be successful?

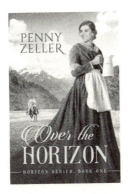

A most unusual proposal...

Made in the USA
Monee, IL
04 December 2022

19600548R00132